GOING UNDER SERIES: BOOK II

GEORGIA CATES

Published by Georgia Cates Books, LLC

Sign-up to join the monthly newsletter for Georgia Cates. You will get the latest news, first-look at teasers, and giveaways just for subscribers.

Editing Services provided by Jennifer Sommersby Young.

Cover Art by J Senter Design

Formatting Services by Indie Formatting Services

ISBN-10: 1475278837

ISBN-13: 978-1475278835

To J, F, and M.
You are my dream come true.

CHAPTER ONE

JESSE BOONE

IT'S TWO WEEKS UNTIL MY FIRST DAY AT EAST FRANKLIN HIGH BUT TODAY, I'M getting a preview of my new teammates. That word suggests we'll be allies but it's impossible for me to think of them in that light. We won't be comrades because they're going to see me for the outsider I am, not one from within their realm of money and privilege.

However, there is one positive note about being transferred from Collinsville to East Franklin. The football coach is serious when it comes to his team and winning the state championship. So am I—being the starting quarterback for the Tennessee state football champions will gain the attention I so desperately need from college scouts.

I'm the epitome of dire straits but I have a plan in place and it's a good one. Make first-string quarterback, win the state championship, and earn a full scholarship to any college. It's the only way I'll get the hell out of this place.

This isn't just football to me. It's my life hanging by a thread.

I join a crowd of guys sitting on the stadium bleachers but keep to myself as I wait to hear what the man standing before us has to say. He introduces himself as Coach Osborne and the man next to him as his assistant, Coach Sheffield. He says everything one would anticipate—the inspiring stuff about this season being the best ever and ensures us we have the ability to take it all the way to the state championship.

"And last but not least … I'll need a copy of your physical from your physician before I can put you on the field."

Bad news. Seeing a doctor requires health insurance and funds I don't have. Even if I can get the money for the exam, my worries are multiplied when I think of the recent injury to my shoulder. What will I do if a doc won't release me to play? My arm isn't a hundred percent. I still have a lot of pain. I just deal with it, though, rather than mess with narcotics.

I watch the other players form a line to turn in their paperwork. Some things never change for me. I've spent my entire life raising my hand to tell teachers and leaders that I don't have the supplies I need. Here I am, eighteen years old, still doing the same thing. It's humiliating.

I lift my hand and the head coach gives me a chin lift and points in my direction. "Yes?"

"I haven't had a physical. I'm a transfer student and didn't know I needed one since they weren't required at my old school." It's true. I had no idea of the requirement but it wouldn't have mattered even if I'd known.

"You can't practice until you're released by a doctor and I have the paperwork on file. What's your name?"

"Jesse Boone."

He lifts his clipboard and begins writing. "Where have you transferred from?"

I sigh with disappointment. I already know it wouldn't take long for my new classmates to figure me out, but I'd hoped I might get a fair shake before my true roots were exposed. I could forget that now. Everyone knows only poor kids go to Collinsville. "Collinsville."

Coach Osborne doesn't look up from his clipboard. "What position?"

"Starting quarterback for the last two years."

A small crowd of guys erupt into laughter and playfully punch and shove a teammate. "Looks like you've got some competition, Henderson."

Henderson, as in Forbes Henderson. I recognize the name from his fifteen minutes of fame during last season's playoffs.

He sizes me up with narrowed eyes and I return the gaze. I can't have him believing I'm afraid of a little competition, least of all from him since he choked and lost the trophy for EF.

Coach continues taking notes. "You throw right or left, Boone?"

"Both."

He grins and his shoulders shake as he laughs under his breath. "Yeah, okay. Which is your better throwing arm?"

This is the moment I've waited for. "I'm ambidextrous. I can throw about sixty yards from both."

I hear murmurs among the crowd before a voice yells out, "He's full of it."

"Only one way to find out." Coach motions for me to follow him onto the field and then tosses me a football. The crowd of disbelievers gathers on the sideline. Their stances and laughter say it all—they think I'm a joke. But we'll see who's laughing when they see I'm telling the truth.

"Cooper, you can be his receiver." A preppy guy in a polo and expensive jeans sprints to the end zone.

Coach Osborne is standing with his arms crossed, waiting. "Show us what you've got."

I walk out to the center of the field and stretch both of my arms. My left shoulder feels a little tight and I pray it doesn't let me down.

I signal the guy called Cooper to start running and I throw the ball with my left arm, spiraling a little more than sixty yards. The pass is completed perfectly when Cooper catches it. I breathe a sigh of relief.

Coach Osborne nods, his face giving away nothing, although I think I detect a lift of his brow behind his sunglasses. "Okay. Show me what you can do with your right arm."

Cooper hurls the ball back and I rotate my right shoulder in preparation. When ready, I cue Cooper to start running and then I watch the football spiral toward him. The pass is perfect, beautiful even, and I give silent thanks to both arms for not failing me.

"Impressive. I think you just found a place on this team. I need you to get a physical as soon as possible so I can put you on the field to practice."

Shit. How am I going to pull that off? "Yes, sir."

"Until you're cleared, I want you observing the team to see how they work together."

"Yes, sir."

I take a seat on the bench while the others dress out. I'm looking down at my worn Nikes as I wait, speculating about how I'll buy new cleats. Mine are in bad shape.

I hear the players returning to the field and look up just in time to catch the football Henderson just threw at my head. "Hey, Collinsville. Better get used to sitting on the bench because that's where your game time will be spent."

I should keep my mouth shut and lie low, but I see his malicious grin and I can't resist. "Am I confused or are you not the quarterback that got his ass handed to him in the state championship game last season?"

My retaliation earns some cackles from the team, but not Henderson. He's about to retaliate but misses his chance when Coach walks onto the field behind him. I'm not stupid enough to think this is over—only postponed.

Practice begins and I immediately see that the team functions differently than the Collinsville team. It's only the first practice, but I recognize how well they perform together. No wonder they went to the finals. Their familiarity with one another makes me nervous about finding my place among them, both on and off the field.

The kicker takes a water break and sits on the bench next to me. "Collinsville, huh? I hear things are pretty bad there. How'd you manage to not get shot?"

I'm shocked he's speaking to me like a human being, rather than like the trash everyone assumes us to be, but he's right. The kids at Collinsville are out of control. Drugs, knives, guns, you name it and it's going on there. "Just lucky, I guess."

He offers his hand. "I'm Dane Wickham."

I shake his hand firmly. "Jesse Boone."

"Yeah, I heard. You've got some mad skills. How'd you train yourself to throw with both arms so well?" He gulps water while waiting for my answer.

The truth is that being ambidextrous is the only genetic perk I got from my worthless parents, but there's no way I'm going there with this guy. "I didn't train myself to do it. I've always been able to use either of my hands equally."

"Well, it's really cool and we're glad to have you on our team, even if Henderson is acting like a dick."

I can't help but be amused. "Thanks. I'm glad to be here. My old coach didn't give a shit about the team or if we ever won a single game. He just showed up because it was a part of his job he couldn't dodge."

"Hey, water boy!" Henderson yells at me from across the field. "Bring me something to drink. I'm thirsty since I'm out here playing and not sitting on the bench."

"What an asshole." I lift my arm high into the air and flip him off.

Dane laughs. "That's Forbes Henderson. He's our quarterback from last year, but I'm guessing you've already figured that out."

"Yeah, I know who he is."

"He's showing his ass because he knows you just bumped him from the starting position. Ignore him."

Does this guy think I'm concerned about that jackoff? "I hope I don't look like I'm worried, 'cause I'm not."

The guy laughs. "Yeah, I might have gathered that." He takes another gulp of water. "I can already tell that this is going to be an interesting season."

Coach Sheffield is standing on the field with his hands on his waist. "Wickham, you kicking today or what?" he yells from the end zone.

"'Or what' means running extra laps after practice. I'll catch you later."

He talks like we'll be hanging out or something. "Sure. Whatever."

Practice lasts three hours, and watching Henderson throw makes me itch to get out there with the team—my team. I'm ready for them to see what I'm made of. More importantly, I need to show Henderson that it's time for him to move over.

When practice ends, I walk toward the field house so I can speak privately with Coach Osborne about the required physical, but Henderson blocks the doorway. The whole team is watching us from within and I know this is it—the defining moment where everyone will form his opinion of me based on how I handle this situation.

"That's a snazzy little trick you can pull but don't be under the impression that you're gonna walk into the starting quarterback position. I'm not giving it up."

I can't afford to be labeled a troublemaker by my coaches so I don't respond. I attempt to step around him. It's clearly not the response he's looking for so he shoves his shoulder into mine, causing me to stumble backward. "Did you hear me, boy?"

His words and sneer trigger something in me—a reminder of the way my mom's boyfriend, Wayne, would smirk in that brief moment before he raised his fist to hit me.

I grab Forbes by his practice jersey and yank him from the doorway, slamming his back against the wall of the concrete-block field house. "Never touch me again. Understood?"

"Do we have a problem already, guys?" Coach is standing in the doorway of his office, arms folded over his chest, waiting for an answer.

I straighten Forbes's jersey and pat him on the arm. "No, Coach. I think there's a crystal clear understanding between us. Don't you agree, Henderson?"

He narrows his eyes more, his lip hinting at a snarl. "I believe

Boone and I understand each other perfectly."

"Glad to hear it. Now get out of here, Forbes." He dismisses him with the wave of his hand. "Boone, I need to see you in my office."

Perfect. I'm the one that will take the ass-chewing. It shouldn't come as a surprise since it's only natural that the rich kid gets away with everything.

I follow Coach and he tells me to have a seat before he shuts the door. That's never a good sign.

I inhale deeply and swallow hard, my best poker face on, a mask for the fear I have of being told to get out because he doesn't have a place on his team for Collinsville troublemakers.

"Do you realize the kind of exceptional talent you have?"

Wow. That's not what I was expecting to hear. A sigh of relief escapes my chest.

"Colleges dream of getting their hands on someone like you. The gift you have is rare, even in the NFL."

I'm not being thrown off the team. I can breathe again. "I really hope a college will want me because I have to get a full scholarship." I hear the desperation in my voice. Shame rises to my face.

Coach looks me over while leaning back in his chair. He's judging me. It's a look I've seen all of my life. "Have you not gotten the physical because you didn't know about it, or can you not afford it?"

Every important time in my life has always come to this—the part where I'm forced to admit I have nothing. "I didn't know it was a requirement." I consider leaving it at that but decide there's no point in not telling the whole truth. "But even if I had, I can't afford it right now."

He brings his hand to his chin and rubs it, saying nothing. I'm afraid he's about to ask about my parents and home life, so I attempt to redirect. "But I can talk to my boss about an advance on my paycheck."

He grabs a scratchpad from the desk and begins writing. "My wife's brother is a physician and this is the address for his office. I'll let him know you'll be coming this afternoon."

There's no way I can get the advance by then. "But I don't have the money for a doctor's visit today. I just need a little time."

"Ronnie will see you at no charge."

What? No one had ever cut me a break in my life—except for my boss, Earl—so what was the catch? "Why would a doctor I don't know do that for me?"

"Because I want you on my team. The sooner I get you practicing, the quicker I can see exactly what I can do with you."

I can't recall a time in my life when anyone wanted me. "Thank you."

I no longer have the burden of worrying about how to pay for a doctor's visit but I'm plagued with a new stressor. I don't enjoy feeling like a charity case and I worry the other guys will find out I got a free physical. They'll rag me forever if that happens.

"No worries. The team will never know." It's as if Coach can read my mind.

I nod, too choked to speak.

I leave the field house and my new team members are hanging out in the parking lot with more than a dozen girls—beautiful girls in matching athletic shorts and T-shirts that read EFHS. They must be the cheerleading squad.

My new arch-rival is holding hands with the hottest girl in the group, a petite little thing with a tiny waist wearing a tight shirt that shows off her perfect tits. Her long, auburn hair is pulled into the classic cheerleader ponytail.

I walk to my truck, totally expecting a cheap shot from Henderson, and he doesn't disappoint. "Hey, superstar. Are you still waiting for the NFL to send your first paycheck so you can buy a ride that doesn't come from the junkyard?"

He laughs. The girl by his side jerks her hand from his and slaps him across the chest. I'm disappointed it isn't his face but she has no reason to defend me. Frankly, I'm surprised she didn't join him in humiliating me since they're cut from the same cloth.

I open the squeaky door to my old, beat-up truck and curse

myself for not lubing it. "Wow, Henderson. That's a creative line for someone who just got bumped to second string."

I slam the door before he has the opportunity to belittle me further in front of the cheerleaders. My hand on the key, I hesitate, praying the engine doesn't stall as it often does. Luck is with me when it starts without a hiccup on the first try.

Forbes Henderson looks in my direction as I drive past. I leave knowing this rivalry between us is only beginning.

CHAPTER TWO

CLAIRE DEVERAUX

"Claire! Please, hurry up. Payton is here and you don't want to be late on your first day," my mom yells from downstairs.

"Great," I mutter as I sling my short, ivory floral dress over my head. Time to put it in overdrive.

I don't have time to braid my hair, so I twist a front section and pull it to the side, pinning it with a pair of brown bobby pins. The clock tells me Payton is going to kill me.

Tardiness is the story of my life. It's never my intention to be late but I'm forever rushing. I must've been genetically engineered this way because it isn't possible for me to get anywhere on time. "Payton, give me another minute and I'll be right down."

I spray myself with a soft peach and jasmine body spray and quickly moisturize my legs and arms. Tardy or not, there's no way I'm showing up dry and ashy on my first day of school.

I hate thumbing a ride, even if it is with my best friend. I curse the ignoramus who backed into my car at the mall, leaving a huge dent in the bumper. I hope the body shop will have it repaired sooner than projected so I'm not dependent upon Payton all week.

Once satisfied with my outfit, I grab my new backpack filled with fresh school supplies and haul ass downstairs. As expected, my mom and Payton are in the kitchen sipping coffee. "Sorry I'm running late."

"That's why I got here early, so I can motivate you to move faster." My best friend knows me too well. "At least you look fantastic. The scarf is the perfect touch for that dress."

Payton gets up from the kitchen table and I motion for her to rotate. She's wearing a coral top with printed leggings and the boots we bought on our back-to-school shopping spree. "You look pretty magnificent yourself."

"Get moving. You can admire one another in the car."

Mom gives me a quick hug. "I have group late tonight and your dad is on call, so you'll have to fend for yourself for dinner."

"No problem." And it's not. I've been doing it for years.

Payton drives faster than she should. "I'll be on time the rest of the week. Promise."

"Yeah, we'll see about that."

My phone buzzes with Forbes's tone. I dig in my purse for the noisemaker, waiting to hear Payton's commentary. She never fails to be entertaining.

She reaches to turn down the music. "Let me guess. The guy who thinks only with the head between his legs wants you to come and blow his mind before homeroom."

"You would say something like that."

Forbes has become such a jealous control freak the last couple of weeks, so I'm not surprised by his text asking where I'm at. "He's looking for me because he's afraid I'll talk to another guy."

"Trouble in paradise?" I don't mistake the hope in her voice.

"I think he's scared I'm going to dump him since he isn't starting quarterback anymore." I regret the words as soon as they're out—I know she'll use them against him. "But don't you dare say a word to him about it."

Payton sighs. "Your boyfriend's insecurities are highly unattractive."

Yeah, tell me about it.

"His fears speak volumes about the way he views you. He sees you as shallow if he's afraid you'll dump him for the Collinsville guy who took his position."

I feel like I should defend him. He is my boyfriend, after all. "I don't know exactly what he's thinking, but please try to cut him some slack. He's not used to losing."

"No shit, Sherlock. Forbes is a brat who always gets his way, but his inability to see that he's not it anymore is incredibly unappealing. He's stuck thinking he's still the superstar, but honey, he lost that spot when he got bumped by the new kid."

None of this is news to me; it's all Forbes talks about. Losing his position to the skank from Collinsville—that's how he phrases it. I thought he'd eventually get over his demotion but after two weeks, he still hasn't accepted it.

"So, what is the hot new quarterback's name?"

"I don't know. I haven't heard Forbes refer to the guy as anything that didn't include profanity. Whatever you do, please don't call him 'hot new quarterback' in front of Forbes."

"Screw Forbes Henderson. I'll tell him myself that the new guy is a sexy mother-scratcher and I dare him to say anything about it."

Oh, lordy. She'll totally do it.

Forbes is humiliated about losing his spot, and today he'll have to face everyone at school for the first time since it happened. He's certain the student body will be laughing behind his back, but I don't think that'll be the case. Let's be honest. No one really cares who the starting quarterback is as long as the football team is winning.

The whole pity-party attitude is a complete turnoff. I don't bring it up because I'm supposed to be the perfect, supportive girlfriend, but the truth is I'm running a little low in the slack department. If he keeps it up, I'll be forced to say something, especially if he tries to use it again as an excuse to get in my pants.

"Please don't jack around with my boyfriend today." I don't think I can stand it if he wallows any deeper.

She huffs dramatically and rolls her eyes. "What would be the fun in that?"

"Do it for me, Payton. Please."

"Ugh!" She groans. "Okay, I won't jack with him, but please know it goes against my better judgment to not take advantage of him during his ego's fragile time."

My best friend and boyfriend hate each other and it stresses me to no end. "Yes, I'm totally aware of how painful this must be for you."

"You have no idea."

"Maybe you should hook up with the new guy and then the two of you could both kick Forbes while he's down."

"That almost sounds like a great plan since he's hot as hell, but you know he's not my type." Her tone is condescending.

"You don't know him so how could you be so positive that he's not your type?"

"Umm ... he's the poor type and besides that, I would never date a guy from Collinsville."

She's being a total bitch. "He's not from Collinsville anymore."

She looks over at me and lifts her flawlessly plucked brow. "Well, he was at one point and that tells me all I need to know. He's not my kind of boyfriend material."

I can't agree with her less. "Wow, you are really acting like a stuck-up wench, Payton."

"My parents would have a total come apart if I brought a boy like that home with me. That big-ass tattoo covers his whole upper arm and that would not fly with the parents because nothing less than a long sleeve is going to hide it."

I like his ink. "So what? A tattoo doesn't make him a bad person."

"It speaks of his character, Claire. Seriously, what kind of high school kid has tattoos like that? He looks like he's been in prison— maybe the big house for hot convicts—but you know I don't do the tattooed bad-boy thing. I'm into preppy guys who drive their expensive cars to boutiques to buy me luxurious gifts."

I didn't dare tell Payton that I think the new kid's tattoo sleeve is the sexiest thing I've ever seen. She'll think I'm out of my mind. No one, including her, could fathom that the perfect Claire Elizabeth Deveraux could possibly find all that badness alluring. But I'm not the perfect Claire everyone thinks I am. Payton knows my imperfections far better than anyone, but even she doesn't realize how badly I want to burst out of the protective cocoon placed around me by everyone in my life.

CHAPTER THREE

JESSE BOONE

ASIDE FROM DANE WICKHAM, I MADE NO FRIENDS BY WALKING ONTO THE East Franklin football team. Practice has been tense at best. My teammates are Forbes's buddies so they all resent me, but it's of little consequence. I'm not here to make friends.

Today is my first day at East Franklin and I'm awake two hours before my alarm goes off. I spend the time staring at my ceiling, riddled with dread. On one hand, I'd rather have my ass whipped than transfer to EFHS with its rich, snobby kids. On the other, it could quite possibly be my only way off this hopeless path I call my life.

The droopy ceiling panels over my bed are another reminder of how different I am from the kids attending EFHS. I guarantee none of them are lying in bed looking at a ceiling threatening to cave in, so it's very easy to refrain from misleading myself into believing I will fit in with any of them.

I force myself out of bed and go to the kitchen for some breakfast. I'm not shocked to discover that someone has eaten almost all the cereal I bought for my breakfast this week. I take the milk carton from the fridge and there's barely enough left to wet the few tablespoons of corn flakes in my bowl. Shit. I just went to the grocery store yesterday and all the food I bought with my own money is gone.

My grandmother, Rita, sits at the dinette set drinking strong black coffee and smoking a filterless Camel cigarette—something she never runs out of—and I recognize the look on her face. She's hungover.

Her buddies partied here last night, keeping me awake. I didn't bother to look at the clock when I heard the slamming of car doors well into the morning hours but I was grateful for their departure.

Her asshole friends smoked pot and then ate all of my groceries when they got the munchies. Sons of bitches.

I notice several plastic bags of marijuana on the table and I'm able to predict what's coming. I eat in silence, staring into my cereal bowl, so I can avoid looking at the dope. I hope and pray Rita's orders won't come. Not today. Please make someone else do it today.

She alternates between slurping steaming coffee and sucking on a cigarette with her permanently puckered lips. Every puff she takes causes a smacking sound. It's annoying as hell. She knows it irritates me so she makes a game of it. The old bitch purposely turns the television off so I'm forced to endure the sound.

I have two more bites of cereal remaining when she points toward the dope. She uses her hand holding the cigarette as though it's some kind of magic fairy wand. "I want you to sell all of these today. Charge extra because those rich kids can afford to pay a little more."

Dysfunctional doesn't even begin to describe my family dynamics. Other kids' grandmothers do grandmotherly things for them, whatever that might be. Maybe baking cookies or knitting them sweaters. Mine? She uses me to sell her dope. It's not like I haven't done it before—it's the same job my mother assigned me before she died.

I don't want to deal for her but we have an arrangement. I sell her dope and she gives me a place to live. It's not ideal but it puts a roof over my head.

I'm surprised she's ordering me to sell on my first day at a new school. It's a stupid move but then I remember that she isn't looking out for my best interests. She's a drug dealer—and a greedy one. "Don't you think I should at least feel out the situation first and find out who's in the market? What if I asked a narc? I'd be up shit creek for sure. I'm eighteen now."

She takes a big drag on her Camel and blows the smoke up into the air. "I don't care where you sell it, just get me some money today if you want to keep staying here." She always threatens to kick me out if I don't sell.

I finish eating and find the sink full of dirty dishes, beer cans covering the counter. I just cleaned the entire house yesterday. Looks like I'll be doing it again after school.

I shove Rita's dope into my backpack before heading into the bathroom for a shower. Dressed and ready to go, I drive slower than the speed limit as I approach East Franklin High School. I dread the looks I'll get when I pull into the lot in my old truck and park next to their expensive Beamers and Benzes. They'll probably move their vehicles out of fear that their luxury cars might catch something from my old jalopy.

I expect problems at this school. It's overpopulated with doctors' and lawyers' kids after the school board redistricted to send the trailer park kids on the south side to Collinsville and replace them with the rich kids from the neighborhoods on the east side of Franklin. I'm not even sure that's legal, but it's what they did five years ago when the new school was built.

It's by accident alone that I'll be attending East Franklin since I was forced to move in with Rita this summer. Although I'm certain EFHS would happily release me, Collinsville refuses to take me back without tuition because we live just within East Franklin's school district.

I don't have the money for tuition and Rita wouldn't part with a dime for me even if she had a million dollars. She's made it very clear I'm unwelcome and the only reason she allows me to stay is because I move her merchandise.

Rita treats me just like Twyla did, so I'm not puzzled by where my mom learned her amazing parenting skills.

I shove the thoughts of my mother out of my head and pull into the parking lot. My nerves are rattled. I hate admitting that—even to myself—because I see it as weakness, so I do the thing I shouldn't in times like these. I light a cigarette. While I sit in the refuge of my truck smoking a much-needed stress reliever, I watch the returning students around me and I'm amazed.

I have ten minutes until my official first day begins. I ponder having another cigarette after I finish the one in my hand but instead take one last, long drag just as a fancy white Lexus pulls into the spot behind me.

I watch my rearview mirror to see what a high schooler driving a Lexus might look like and I'm not shocked when I discover it's a couple of the cheerleaders I've seen practicing on the field—one of them being Forbes Henderson's girlfriend. The driver looks more like a Barbie than the Mattel doll herself. She has long, blond hair and a pair of killer legs made longer by a pair of tall wedge heels. As I muse on how she'll get away with a skirt that short on school grounds, she straightens it and gains a little length. It still isn't enough to pass inspection at Collinsville but maybe East Franklin overlooks short skirts.

Henderson's girlfriend is wearing a short dress and cowgirl boots. Damn, a chick in a dress with boots is hot. It's too bad this one is taken. She dates a total dick and that lets me know a little about who she is as a person. She's with the enemy and therefore against me by association.

With the enemy or not, these girls aren't like the ones I'm used to at my old school. They're untouchable for a guy like me and I'm sure they wouldn't have a problem informing me of that fact.

I watch Henderson's girl in my mirror as she approaches my driver's side. I quickly toss my finished cigarette out the window and I'm overwhelmed by a sudden need to jack with her.

But I'm curious. I've only seen her from a distance so maybe I should talk to her, study her face to face, so I can convince myself she isn't everything I imagine in my head.

With perfect timing, I swing my door open to prevent her passing.

Man, this is going to be fun.

CHAPTER FOUR

CLAIRE DEVERAUX

I DIE A THOUSAND DEATHS WHEN PAYTON PARKS BEHIND THE SEXY BADASS'S junked-out truck. I think she did it on purpose, to evoke a reaction from me.

He's still sitting in the rusted bucket of bolts, either holding a pencil or cigarette in his hand. My suspicion is confirmed when I see him bring it to his lips for a drag, the tip glowing fiery orange.

Gross. I hate cigarettes.

"Why did you have to park behind him?"

"It's an open spot, and a pretty good one considering we're not exactly early." I get it now. This is my punishment for making us late.

Getting out of the car at the same time means I'll be walking into school next to him. That's a problem for me, one I could've avoided if Payton hadn't parked next to him.

She doesn't care about the ruckus this will cause between me and Forbes. Provoking him entertains her, but I'm not certain she understands that her pleasure comes at my expense. "I'm sick of hearing Forbes whine about this guy and I'd like to avoid an argument about him first thing."

"At the risk of repeating myself, screw Forbes. I'm not parking in the back and walking an extra mile in these shoes to spare your boyfriend's insecurities. If you have to explain that, then you should dump his ass."

She's right. I've become a poodle jumping through hoops to keep the peace. It's ridiculous and exhausting.

"Can we at least get ahead of him so I don't have to explain why we're walking into the building together?" I sound like a total wimp.

Payton is checking her makeup in the visor mirror and huffs as she slams it shut. "This is ridiculous but you know that already, right? Your life might revolve around what Forbes Henderson wants, but mine doesn't."

Payton is moving like a snail so I leave her behind. A cigarette butt flicks out of the truck's window and lands in my path. My boyfriend's replacement on the football team swings his door open, preventing my escape, and I stop dead in my tracks. I'm stupid for not taking a detour around his pickup.

He steps out and stomps the butt on the ground before looking at me, grinning. I have to look up to see his face, making me feel very small. He's at least eight inches taller, if not more.

I've stolen glances at him during cheerleading practice over the last two weeks when I was certain Forbes wasn't watching me. I've never clearly seen his face, not even the day Forbes talked shit to him about this truck, so he's been a mystery in my mind.

His helmet and face mask no longer obstruct my view and I now see the proof that he is so much more handsome than I originally guessed. His hair is darker than I thought and spiky on top. His pale blue stare is piercing, his eyes breathtaking, and I have to force myself to not become lost in them.

"Pardon me, princess. I didn't mean to block your way." His voice is velvety smooth, but I don't mistake its coolness. It clearly conveys the contempt he feels for me and that immediately raises my hellcat flag. This guy does not know me and therefore has nothing to base his aversion on.

He's judging me—and making assumptions—just like everyone else in my life.

I'm immediately angry with him for making presumptions about who I am, but I'm far more furious with myself for finding him so captivating. I taste the bitter reaction on my tongue as it manifests in the form of a verbal insult. "Asshole."

He laughs and places his hand over the left side of his chest. "I felt that like a blade straight to my heart."

I'm pissed and the bastard is enjoying it.

I push past him. "Screw you. And my name is not 'princess.' It's Claire. If you're going to insult me, at least have the decency to get my name right."

"I think I'll stick with princess. It suits you better," I hear him call behind me, laughing.

I'm speed walking to get away from him but Payton somehow manages to catch up with me. "Slow your jets, please. I'm in four-inch wedges." I don't apologize since all of this could've been avoided if she'd not purposely parked beside him.

I don't slow my pace. "We're going to be late."

Four-inch heels or not, she hangs next to me. "I'm completely disappointed by the way you executed that performance. You looked like a total amateur."

I can't argue with that. He bested me and I basically rolled over. "Sorry. I went blank."

It was those damn eyes. I got lost looking into them.

"I taught you so much better than that. How can I call you my best friend when you caved so easily?"

"It won't happen again." I'd make damn sure of that because I can't afford to let Forbes see me lose my cool with this guy.

"By the way, you've got something all over your ass."

I twist my upper body and grab the bottom of my dress, pulling it around for inspection. "What is it?"

"Hot new guy's eyes." She laughs. "Sorry. I had to. You walked right into it."

I normally find her jokes and banter entertaining—until they're aimed at me. "He's an asshole and so are you. I think you'd make the perfect pair."

She rolls her eyes. "That lacks creativity. We have to work on your comebacks because you are seriously letting down your slander master."

"I don't need bitch lessons."

She laughs. "Right, because you're such a badass all on your own, 'Miss I Gotta Keep Forbes Happy at My Own Expense.'"

I can't argue with that, and I don't have a comeback. She's right. I need work.

"You're beet red and it's not because you're pissed. You're blushing because you think he's hot."

No way I'm letting her know I like what I see. "Whatever you're smoking has you reality challenged."

"Boy, did he get it wrong when he called you 'princess.' He should've dubbed you Queen of Denial since you'll never admit what's happening here."

How can she so clearly see through me? "I have no idea what kind of nonsense you're talking about."

"I can describe your entire interaction with that guy in one word."

This should be interesting. "What?"

She's grinning. "Foreplay."

CHAPTER FIVE

JESSE BOONE

I watch Claire walk away, admiring the angry sway of her hips in her short floral dress, and I laugh at how well fury suits her. I reluctantly admit to myself that my hopes about her are all wrong. She is all that, plus a whole lot of spunk I didn't expect.

Her auburn hair is longer than it appears when pulled into a ponytail at cheerleading practice. I originally thought her eyes were brown, and they are in the center, but the outer edge is green and unlike any I've seen before.

She got mad as hell when I called her princess, so that must mean I've found the button I'll be pushing at every opportunity.

I've got six minutes until I have to be in homeroom. I could've stayed in my truck to get my nicotine fix instead of jacking with the princess, but it was worth missing a few drags to yank her chain.

Maybe she'll run and tell her boyfriend. I'd love for him to start a fight so I'd have an excuse to stomp his smart ass into the ground. I smile, delighting in the possibility.

Screw it. I light up so I can get a few drags on the walk to class. If I get confronted by a teacher, I'll lie and say I didn't know East Franklin had a no-smoking policy. I flick my cigarette onto the ground and give it a stomp when I get close to the school entrance.

I pop a breath mint as I enter the building and see a dude looking lost as he studies a copy of his class schedule. Guess I'm not the only new kid. I'm glad I came earlier in the week to set up my schedule with the counselor and locate my classes. Saved me from looking dumb like this guy.

I enter Mrs. Garrett's homeroom and take a seat in the back. I slump down in my desk, pretending no one will see me if I slide low enough. I scan the room for the princess and curse to myself when I don't see her. She's the only thing that could've been of interest in this room. I'm curious if I'll have any classes with her.

While I'm staring off into space thinking about the princess, someone sits in the desk next to me. "Hey, Jesse."

I turn at the sound of my name. Dane. My only friend at East Franklin has unexpectedly turned out to be pretty cool, even if he is one of the rich kids.

I give him a nod. "What's up?"

He shrugs. "Nothing that amounts to anything."

I sit up and hunch over the desk. "I hear ya."

Aside from being my only comrade, Dane is likely my only access to the inside scoop on Henderson's girl. "Hey, do you know that chick named Claire?"

He wrinkles his brow. "You must mean Claire Deveraux."

I give him a shrug. "Maybe. I don't know her last name."

"Long brown hair?" He cups his hands against his chest. "And a gorgeous pair of tits you want to bury your face in?"

I want to correct him about her hair color. He's obviously never looked at it in the sun but he has the description of her breasts right on. "That's her."

"What's up? Why are you asking about Claire?"

"I want to know about her and what her deal is."

He studies me before answering. I think he's trying to sort out my motives but he knows the beef between me and Henderson, so it shouldn't be difficult to figure out. "She's Henderson's girl."

There it is—the proof that she isn't just hanging out with that dick. "I know that much."

"Claire is East Franklin's sweetheart. Everyone loves her." Nice. Everyone would know I had upstaged Henderson if I took her from him.

"I don't have to tell you how hot she is. And she's smarter than anyone in our class. She'll be our valedictorian for sure." Hmm … she's intelligent. That could make for a problem if I don't play this right.

"How long have they dated?"

"Since the middle of our sophomore year. Their parents are big buddies, so they're always going on family vacations together." Shit. That could be a problem as well. It means she's loyal.

I bet that bastard is the first and only guy to get in her pants. That could be a wrench in my plan as well since chicks can never get over the one who hits it first.

"I saw you talking to her in the parking lot this morning. You trying to put the moves on her?"

He sounds protective so I can't let him know about the plans I have for her. "Nah, just thought I'd mess with Henderson by talking to her. I figure she'll run and tell him what I said."

"You shouldn't push Forbes. He's a loose cannon. Claire thinks she knows him but he has a side she's never seen. Trust me when I say he's an underhanded dog."

The thought of Forbes being a threat makes me want to laugh. "Dude, I've seen loose cannons, and Forbes Henderson is nothing more than a sparkler from a roadside fireworks stand."

Dane leans forward and lowers his voice. "There's something I need to tell you about him and his pals. I overheard them talking about taking you out so you can't play anymore. I don't know the details, but it's going down sometime before the first game. I think you should tell Coach."

I appreciate the heads-up, but I take care of myself. "No way, dude. I'd rather get my ass kicked than be a snitch."

He's looking at me like I'm stupid. "Whatever. It's your funeral."

Dane's a stand-up guy. I wouldn't put it past him to tell Osborne or Sheffield behind my back. "I mean it. Not a word to Coach. I can handle whatever they dish."

I consider the different scenarios of what taking me out means. Most likely they would try to catch me somewhere outside of school and jump me. Thing is, those little rich punks don't realize they're screwing with the wrong person.

"Thanks for telling me. I know you didn't have to do that. If you hear something else, will you let me know?"

Dane shrugs. "No problem."

CHAPTER SIX

CLAIRE DEVERAUX

I STUPIDLY PLACE MYSELF ON MRS. JENSON'S TARDY RADAR WHEN I BREEZE into class by the skin of my teeth. I attempt to sneak into a seat but only manage to gain the undesirable scrutiny of my new homeroom teacher when I stumble over Griffin Jackson's backpack in the aisle. Griffin quickly reaches for my arm, touching my boob in the process, and saves me from sprawling on my back in front of the entire class.

"Sorry, Claire." I'm not certain if Griffin is apologizing for touching my boob or leaving his backpack in the aisle but the whole thing is my fault. I stumbled because I was still preoccupied by baby blues.

"It's okay."

Old Lady Jenson makes a display of looking down her nose at me as I cross the classroom. I sit next to my friend and fellow cheerleader, Allie Bumphis, and pretend I don't notice Jenson's eyes following me. I perceive her stare for what it is—a nonverbal warning daring me to be late again.

Allie leans in my direction. "I saw you talking to the new quarterback. Do you know him?"

Shit. If she saw me, then who else did? "Nope."

"Then what were you talking about? I'm sure it wasn't Forbes."

What is she insinuating?

I open my mouth to reply and Mrs. Jenson clears her throat. "Ladies, do you have something you'd like to discuss with the class?"

Is this old lady serious? We're seniors, not kindergarteners. Who doesn't let their students talk in homeroom on the first day of school?

I look at Allie and then back to Mrs. Jenson. "No, ma'am."

After hearing the announcements and serving my sentence in homeroom, the bell rings. I race down the hall where I'm guessing I'll find Payton claiming the neighboring lockers we've shared for the previous two years. She's already there, glossing her lips with perfect peach, her signature color, and fluffing her long, blond hair. She smiles as though she likes what she sees—she should because she's beautiful.

She turns and props against her locker. "Have you forgiven me, Claire Bear?"

I have a poor record of staying mad at Payton so she already knows the answer. "No."

"Good, because I have to tell you about my crappy luck. I had to sit next to The Ladies' Man in homeroom."

Marcus Lee was nicknamed "The Ladies' Man" after an old spoof on Saturday Night Live about Leon Phelps, a horny talk show host. The guy is actually proud of the nickname because he thinks it's a compliment. What a tool!

"He's such a creep. He gave me that up-and-down look with those weird grunting and moaning sounds he makes. I feel like I need a morning-after pill and strong antibiotics."

The boy knows how to violate a girl with his eyes alone. I'm glad I won't have to face him first thing every morning. I was tormented with his daily bump-and-grind routine during sophomore year.

It's too bad Payton is facing visual and verbal molestation by

Marcus every morning. "Been there, done that. It's not pretty, but I wish you the best of luck with the horn dog. I got stuck with the tardy Nazi for homeroom."

I'm grabbed from behind and spun in a circle. I briefly make eye contact with the sexy badass's beautiful blues before he makes a snide face and enters Miss Dulaney's calculus class. Good. That means I don't have first period with him.

"Put me down." My feet return to the floor and Forbes plants a kiss on the back of my neck. I whirl around. "You'd better cut that out before Mr. Grisham sees us. You know he doesn't tolerate PDA."

"You worry too much. He's not gonna say anything now that we're seniors."

Forbes's best friend, Cooper, stands next to us. "She's right, Forbes. Grisham's a hard-ass on that PDA stuff. He busted me and Caitlyn Johnson for holding hands back when we were dating."

Forbes doesn't loosen his hold. "Do I look like I care what he says?" He pulls me tighter and pushes my hair to the side to plant another kiss on my neck.

"I don't want to get in trouble on the first day." I look around the hall nervously. The last thing I need is my parents getting a call about inappropriate physical contact at school. My mom already believes that Forbes and I are going at it at every given opportunity. If things went Forbes's way, my mom wouldn't be far off the mark.

He's definitely pressing me harder to go all the way since this whole quarterback thing started. He's been very clear about his growing impatience. He sometimes acts as though it's something I owe him but I'm not ready, and I refuse to give it up just because we've dated for over a year.

The first bell rings and I'm relieved when I'm released without being discovered by Grisham. "What do you have second period, babe?"

"Mrs. Tanner for AP Humanities. It's over in the building where the freshmen classes are."

Forbes shakes his head. "That's so stupid. It's an advanced class stuck in the middle of the ninth grade building. Does it even make sense to mix seniors with little punks that just left junior high?"

I don't mind. I love Mrs. Tanner's classes. "It's not a big deal. I'm excited about being in her class again. We get to do some really cool stuff."

He frowns. "Well, I don't like it because it means I'll miss seeing you between first and second period."

He's acting way more attached than I'd like. "You're such a baby. You'll get over not seeing me." I look at my watch and see that we need to move. "I gotta go. Spanish is on the other end of the hall."

I speed walk for the second time today and make it to Mrs. Santiago's Spanish II class before the bell rings. Cooper waves me over to sit next to him. "I didn't know we had Spanish together. You gonna let me cheat off you?"

"Spanish is my worst subject. You might want to try someone else."

"Your worst grade beats my best any day. We all know you're gonna be valedictorian, so don't pretend like you aren't going to ace this class."

He makes it sound like an A will just be handed to me. "I have to work for my grades. And I'm not the only good student at East Franklin, Coop."

I hate assumptions about who I am. Even friends who know me best don't know the real me. They only see what they want to see. They all think my stellar grades and envied lifestyle come so easy, but they don't. No one gives me credit for the hard work I invest in earning those things on my own. Living up to the expectations of my parents and classmates is exhausting. Some days I think I'd prefer being invisible.

Class begins and Mrs. Santiago introduces herself in Spanish before making us do the same.

Cooper leans forward. "Don't you think there's something a little unfair about a Mexican dude being allowed to take a Spanish class?" He gestures toward a Latino guy sitting in the row closest to the wall. "Maybe I'll cheat off him instead of you."

I shake my head. "You're muy unbien, Cooper."

"I'm gonna have to check with Mrs. Santiago on that one, but I'm pretty sure 'unbien' isn't a word. I'm definitely cheating off him."

The bell rings, signaling the end of our hour-long class. "Damn. That was not at all interesting. I think I might've just had my first boregasm."

I gather my books and we walk out together. "I'd be offended if I didn't know you, but that was classic Cooper."

He sees Payton standing outside the door waiting for me and runs like a scolded dog. "Catch you guys later. I've got some leg to chase on the other end of the hall."

I knew Coop had a huge crush on Payton but I'd never mentioned it to her. My girl wouldn't give him the time of day.

"See you later, masturbator," Payton calls out to him.

"It's really too bad he'll never get out of your friend zone because the two of you would be so perfect," I hint.

"Please tell me that was a thought typo. I could never date that prick after the lame come-on he used when we met."

There is no forgetting it but I still love hearing Payton's impersonation. "Remind me again?"

She rolls her shoulders, readying herself for her Cooper impersonation. "Hey, gorgeous, is that a mirror in your back pocket 'cause I can see myself in your pants."

"I swear it gets better every time you do it."

"Well, do you want me to do my impression of what Jesse Boone said when I confronted him about what happened in the parking lot this morning?"

"Jesse Boone?" It takes a minute but then it registers. That's baby blues's name. "No, you didn't. Tell me you're lying so I don't have to kill you because I really like you not dead."

Who am I kidding? I know she did.

"I wanted to see his reaction and it was just as I suspected." I stand silent. "I hope you believe in the hereafter because that boy is about to be here after you."

CHAPTER SEVEN

JESSE BOONE

I'M IN CALCULUS WAITING FOR CLASS TO BEGIN WHEN CLAIRE'S BLOND FRIEND walks in. She takes a look around and grins when she spies me. What does her smile mean?

She sits in front of me and spins in her desk, extending her hand. "We've not officially met. I'm Payton Archer. And you are?"

Her hotness level is flaming but she doesn't impress me nearly as much as Claire. I note her perfectly manicured hand before taking it in mine. "Jesse Boone."

She wastes no time cutting straight to the chase. "So, Jesse Boone, what kind of move was that you tried to put on Claire in the parking lot?"

I laugh out loud. "That was not a move and if she thinks it was, then Henderson is seriously lacking in the skills department."

She smiles. "I won't disagree about Forbes and his skills, but I'm calling bullshit. I know the game better than your crotch knows the palm of your hand. I definitely saw a move, so I'm giving you the luxury of a warning. Do not mess with Claire because of what's going on between you and Forbes. Do we have an understanding?"

I lean forward and whisper, "Do you suffer from restless lip syndrome? Because they make medication for that." I'm surprised to see a smile spread in place of the scowl I expected.

Our calculus teacher, Miss Dulaney, stands at the front of the classroom but Payton is sure to get the last word. "You might score touchdowns on the football field, but you can forget about getting into Claire's end zone."

Wow. That's my second warning of the day to not mess with Claire and it's only second period. Unbeknownst to these people, to warn me against something is to dare me.

I GRAB A SEAT IN HUMANITIES, one among only seven students, and regret agreeing to take it without finding out what it's all about first. I look around the classroom and take in all the weird paraphernalia on the walls.

I look to the only other guy in the class. "Hey, dude, what kind of class is this?"

"It's AP Humanities with Mrs. Tanner." His tone is as dull as his khaki shirt and pants.

"But what is humanities? Are we gonna be doing weird stuff in here or what?"

By the expression on the kid's face, I realize too late that he and I are not kindred spirits simply because we're the only males in the room. "Humanities doesn't refer to one particular subject. It is the study of many things such as English, literature, grammar, writing, and composition. It also includes history, art, culture, and philosophy and the relationships between them all and how they contribute to our lives and society. Think of it as the total opposite of math and science."

What have I gotten myself into? "That means we'll be doing weird shit, right?"

He shakes his head and looks irritated by my lack of enthusiasm. "How'd you get in this class, anyway? Shouldn't you be with the other meathead jocks?"

"Probably." Well, at least this guy isn't clumping me into the

Collinsville poor-kids group. He's discriminating against me for an entirely different reason—athleticism. I'll take that any day.

I'm contemplating how I'll tell the counselor I want to drop this class when I look up and see Claire the princess walk through the door. She breaks into a huge smile when she sees the teacher and walks over to give her a hug. When the reunion concludes, Claire takes the seat in front of me, failing to recognize that I am the person sitting behind her. Perfect.

Mrs. Tanner casually walks to the front of her desk and plants herself. "I believe everyone is acquainted with the exception of our new transfer student, Jesse Boone."

Claire's back stiffens in her desk. Her reaction to my name makes me happy because it means she knows who I am and I've successfully managed to get under her skin. Mission accomplished.

"Since we're a small class, I want everyone to introduce themselves to Jesse, but first we're rearranging these desks. Those I've taught before know forward facing doesn't work for me. It's crucial that you see one another during discussion time, so let's start with a circle. If that doesn't work out, we'll try facing pairs since we'll be dividing into groups of two the majority of the time."

We stand to move our desks and I notice Claire stealing a glance in my direction. I give her a big shit-eating grin to let her know it doesn't go unnoticed. I like this circle thing very much; she'll have nowhere to hide.

After everyone introduces themselves to me, Mrs. Tanner stands. "Humanities isn't like other classes you've taken. You'll be given the opportunity to expand your vision and imagination by learning to recognize creativity when you see it. This means being able to see it in ourselves as well as in others. Freeing our inner potential for creativity, self-criticism, and self-condemnation is important."

And there it is, ladies and gentlemen. The weirdness has begun.

She continues, "All too often we reject our own creative impulses and actions, but today I have an exercise for you using key ingredients to contribute to creative thinking. I have six listed on the board. I want you to choose a partner and then the two of you will select one element to creatively get to know one another better."

I look around as the others split off into pairs. I'm pleased when I see I'll be coupled with Claire. And without even trying.

I feel like rattling her cage a little. "Princess, should I consider it a bad sign that no one wants to be your partner?"

"I've already told you my name is Claire and who says they don't want to be my partner? Maybe they don't want to be yours. Ever think of that?" she counters.

"Nope. That's not the thought that crossed my mind."

She huffs as a spoiled brat does and then turns to look at the board. "Which element do you want? Recognizing patterns?"

"No, and I don't want 'making connections' or 'taking advantage of chance,' either."

"Agreed. I'm not making a connection with you or letting you take advantage of anything. What about 'taking risks'?" Maybe I should have named her Viper instead of Princess—she has an awfully sharp tongue.

"It's a no-go on 'taking risks.'" I take risks every day and I'm not in the sharing mood.

"That leaves 'challenging assumptions' or 'seeing in new ways.'"

"Princess's choice," I offer.

"'Seeing in new ways,' it is."

After we choose our ingredient, Mrs. Tanner gives us an envelope with a specific topic to discuss. "Preconceived notions: your partner has one about you, so change it by making him or her see you in a new way. Be creative."

Wrong. I don't want the pretty princess to see me as anything but what I am. That's what's going to make it so grand when I steal her from Henderson and hand her back after I've done everything I want with her.

"What's up with that bullshit?"

She smirks. "Well, this exercise is already complete because you just confirmed my preconceived notion about you instead of changing it."

"What exactly is your preconceived notion about me, princess?" This should be good.

"The exercise doesn't say I have to identify what my preconceived notion is. It says I have one and you must attempt to change it by making me see you in a new way. So go for it. Make me see you in a different light because right now, it's not so delightful."

"You think I find you delightful? I call you a princess and you called me an asshole. Princess, positive. Asshole, negative."

"Oh, yeah! You mean princess in the most complimentary way." She rolls her eyes and they flutter. "I know what you think of me so I don't need you to explain."

"Okay, change my mind," I challenge. "Help me see you in a way other than being a pampered princess."

She hesitates and I'm certain she's choosing her words carefully. "My name is Claire Deveraux. Not princess. Not goody-goody. Not Miss Perfection. Not Forbes Henderson's girlfriend. People assume I'm handed everything on a silver platter because my parents are compensated well for their hard work. My life isn't simple or easy and I'm a real person with real problems." She stops and I wait for the punch line.

"Go on. You aren't finished yet."

She clears her throat. "I can never be myself because it isn't what everyone expects. I feel trapped, like it's never okay to be me because who I really am will disappoint those around me."

Instead of embracing her life as the pretty princess, she's whining about it. That just pisses me off. She should try living the way I do and then tell me when it isn't okay to be Claire Deveraux.

There's never been a single day in my life when I wanted to be Jesse Boone. Not one. While growing up, the best I could hope for was to not get my ass beat by my mom's boyfriend. In my book, that was a good day.

This chick is one of the hottest girls I've ever seen, but her pity party is a complete turnoff and only proves she is the pampered princess I pegged her for. "Are you serious or are you messing with me?"

A look of fury envelops her face. "I'm totally serious."

Oh, it's on now. "Tell me a time in your life when it has truly sucked being Claire Deveraux. Name a time when you were cold or hungry and there was no food to eat or warm coat to wear."

She looks down at her desk. "You have everything going for you. You come from a wealthy family. I can take one look at the way you're dressed and know that your boots cost more than my truck. I've already heard you're incredibly smart and expected to be the class valedictorian." She looks up at me and I can't identify what it is I see in her hazel eyes. "And you're gorgeous—probably one of the most beautiful girls I've ever seen."

Damn. Where did that come from?

She looks at me a moment before turning away. "You're just like all the others. You only see the outside and what you want to see."

"Show me something different and maybe I'll think you're something besides a spoiled brat."

She shakes her head. "I'm done. My turn's over so you're next."

I considered her probable assumptions about me and decide to roll with it. I don't have much of an argument for changing them since most are likely true.

"I'll pass." I know that won't get me off the hook but I do it to annoy her.

"Not an option."

"I'm not going to say anything that will change your mind about who I am, so this exercise may be deemed unsuccessful."

"This is an assignment, so you have to tell me something even if it's proving you're an asshole."

"What do you want to hear?"

She looks up at me through long, dark lashes. "Tell me something real."

She almost looks like she cares.

She must be jacking around, trying to convince me to tell her personal things about myself—stuff she can tell Henderson. "My name is Jesse Boone, aka asshole. I'm a loser from Collinsville like everyone thinks. I don't come from a rich family like all of you spoiled brats and it completely defines me and what I'm capable of doing, so I'll never amount to anything because it's what I've been told my whole life." Let her believe I don't have aspirations for something better since I'm sure that's what she thinks anyway.

Her shock meter doesn't budge.

"So, does this change how you see me or validate exactly what you think you already know about me?"

"Yes, it validates you're an asshole and no, it doesn't change what I think about you at all."

Perfect.

CHAPTER EIGHT

CLAIRE DEVERAUX

I THINK ABOUT JESSE BOONE'S INCONSISTENCY AS I WALK TO MY LOCKER. HE was unguarded and sincere for a brief moment when he temporarily forgot to be a jerk. The assignment was successful for a minute, when I caught a potential new glimpse of him, but then I watched him transform back to his former asshole self.

Which Jesse is the real one?

The moment I realized he was sitting behind me, I felt breathless. When I tried to sneak a peek at him, he saw me and grinned. Him knowing I was checking him out made me want to die right then and there.

He's probably the most handsome boy I've ever seen. I struggle with labeling him a boy; the way his black T-shirt stretches taut across his chest and around his muscular arms clearly proves why the term doesn't fit.

As I swap out my books, I remember how Jesse's black tattoo peeked out of his sleeve as he reached to pick up a pencil from the floor.

I let out an embarrassing squeal when Payton begins speaking behind me. Mr. Grisham is in the hall and gives us that keep it down, ladies look.

I spin on my heels and glare at my best friend. "Don't sneak up on me like that."

"I did not sneak up on you. You just didn't hear me because you were off in la-la land with Jesse Boone."

I look around to make sure no one is listening. "I was not," I lie. "And keep it down. Someone could hear you and get the wrong impression."

"My dear Claire, you are the worst liar ever. You practically have a lie meter across your forehead, and right now it's registering that you just told a big fat one."

No matter how hard I try, I can never keep anything from Payton. "Okay. You caught me but I was only thinking about him because we have second period together and had to be partners on a class exercise."

"Your lie meter is registering a half-truth because you were thinking about him as a partner that included exercise, but not a class assignment. Maybe something more along the lines of the horizontal tango."

Omigod. I wish she'd shut up before someone hears her big mouth. "No, I'm not."

She puts her palms up. "Hey, I'm just keeping it real."

Forbes walks up beside me. "What are we keeping real? Payton's need for penicillin?" Oh, lordy. Here we go.

Payton slams her locker and spins to face my boyfriend. "I may pimp slap you if you insist on talking."

The job of refereeing these two is exhausting.

I point at Payton. "You. U.S. history. Now." I shove Forbes in the direction of his next class. "Go before you exceed the limits of her restraint to push her pimp-slap button."

We part without incident and I join Payton in the back row of Mr. Buckley's U.S. history class. We're waiting for the lecture to begin when Jesse walks in. He takes a brief look around the room for a seat and I silently pray he'll sit on the opposite side of the room. But then he sees me and the empty desk in front of me.

Don't do it. Don't sit next to me.

He does.

He peers over his shoulder. "You took my seat."

I make a show of searching the desk. "Umm … I'm sorry. I don't see your name anywhere."

He turns and begins writing across the top of my desktop. The smart ass is writing his name on my desk.

"That's called destruction of school property." I sound so uptight. No wonder people think I'm goody-goody.

He laughs before turning around in his seat. I look down to erase his name and see that he has written, "You should smile more."

What a strange thing to say to me. Or write. "Why?"

He speaks over his shoulder again. "Because it looks good on you."

There it is again—the mysterious Jesse Boone. His inconsistency makes me think about him during class. I can't concentrate on a thing Mr. Buckley says.

I see Payton swat her hand out of the corner of my eye. I turn to see what she wants. She mouths the word "foreplay." I give her the finger. Thank God Jesse has his back to us. I'd die if he knew Payton was accusing us of flirting.

I hope Jesse doesn't turn around to say anything else because I don't need another reason to think about him.

When class is over, he leaves without speaking or looking in my direction. Although it's what I want, I find myself feeling disappointed. And foolish. What kind of game is he playing with me?

I barely make it to my locker before Payton is on me. "I dare you to tell me he's not hot for you."

Deny. Deny. Deny. "Jesse isn't hot for me. He's just a guy having a little fun with a princess. That's all."

"No way. I see what's happening here."

I'd love for her to shed some light on the situation because I don't have a clue. "There's nothing going on."

"He may call you princess but he damn sure doesn't treat you like one. And you love it."

Her theory is ... ridiculous. "He's a total ass to me. Why would I enjoy that?"

Payton is laughing and I think it's at me. "Omigod, Claire, you can be incredibly dense for someone so smart. Do I really have to spell it out?"

"Please do because I have no idea where you're going with this nonsense."

"Jesse probably sees you as a spoiled rotten little princess. Considering where he's from, I bet he can't stand those kinds of girls and it's pissing him off that he can't help himself from being turned on by you." Hmm ... maybe that explains why he's so mercurial toward me.

"And you ..." Oh, lordy. Now she's going to diagnose me. "This is the first time you've ever met a guy who didn't place you on a pedestal and you're completely fascinated. It just so happens that he's one good-looking mother-scratcher—but with a big-ass tattoo."

I'll only admit it to myself but I do experience something different when I'm around Jesse. It's intriguing. I love how he doesn't automatically treat me like everyone else in my world.

"It's all part of the game, Claire. Don't get me wrong. I'm proud of your newfound sketchiness but there's one thing you must remember: Jesse's the kind of guy you play with for a little fun, not the kind you fall in love with."

I TAKE the table at the back in physics and put my head down. Payton has given me way too much to consider. My head feels like it might explode.

I feel a warm hand on the back of my neck. "Hey, babe, is everything okay? You feel sick?" The sound of Forbes's voice surprises me and I lift my head to find him sitting next to me. I forgot we had this class together.

"I don't feel great," I lie.

What is up with me? I never lie—so why am I lying to Payton and Forbes? I lean back in my seat and in walks the reason I'm suddenly able to spout off deception at the drop of a hat.

"Great, here comes the Collinsville skank," Forbes whines.

Jesse is walking next to Gretchen, better known as the penivore, and the only table left in the class is the one directly in front of me and Forbes. Perfect.

It's difficult to concentrate on Mrs. Bishop's lecture since I'm forced to watch Gretchen flirt shamelessly with Jesse. She leaves little to the imagination, letting him know he can have it from her any way he wants it at any time. It's disgusting. And I bet he takes her up on the offer.

And I'm disgusting for being preoccupied with him while my long-term boyfriend sits unsuspecting, right next to me. Man, I'm a sucky girlfriend.

I recall the perfect plans Forbes and I have made for our future and resolve that this senseless interest in Jesse Boone must stop. In the end, I will be with Forbes. Jesse will screw Gretchen just like half the guys at East Franklin and then he'll move on to the next skanky whore. My temporary interest in him is only a minor technicality I plan to sweep neatly under the rug—as soon as I find a broom.

CHAPTER NINE

JESSE BOONE

I'M NOT INTERESTED IN GRETCHEN—AT LEAST NOT TODAY. I'VE BEEN THERE and done that kind of girl before but I admit, it's always nice to have a backup plan.

The rest of my classes were boring without having Claire around to taunt. I thought the torment wouldn't end—but it did—and now I'm on the field, warming up while waiting on the rest of the team to show for practice.

Beside me, Dane stretches his legs. "So, what did you think of your first day at East Franklin?"

What can I say? It's nice being in a school with kids who haven't shown up on my doorstep to buy dope. I like not being known as the kid with the mom who can hook you up with whatever kind of drug you want.

My reply to Dane's question is still hanging in the air when I notice the cheerleaders arriving on the field for practice. Claire briefly makes eye contact. "Definitely different from my old school. The view here is much nicer."

"I get that you want to mess with Forbes, but Claire's a nice girl. Don't do anything to hurt her."

There it is—another warning. "I'm not some kind of animal. I'm just messing with her to get Henderson riled up. You've seen some of the things he's done to me and you know firsthand what he's planning. There's no harm to her by talking. What's your deal? You into her or something?"

"Our parents are friends so I've known her a long time." He gets up and kicks an imaginary ball. "Forget I said anything. You're going to do whatever you want anyway."

As much as I hate Henderson, I don't want a dispute with my only friend. Just as I'm about to promise Dane I'll leave Claire out of my warfare with Henderson, the devil himself walks up and starts in on me. "Hey, Collinsville skank, do you spank the monkey ambidextrously?"

I should take the high road. But I don't because I've never backed down a day in his life. "Your girlfriend wasn't complaining last night about what I could do ambidextrously."

Our teammates erupt into laughter.

If there's one thing I've learned, it's how to dodge a clenched hand coming at my face. It's like child's play when I sidestep Forbes's swinging fist. "I believe that is the slowest sucker punch I've ever seen."

"Henderson! Boone! In my office now!" Coach yells from the doorway of the field house.

I plop down into the chair in his office. Although I didn't start it, I feel badly for causing Coach Osborne trouble after he helped me out with my physical. "This stops now! No more fighting—verbally or physically. I don't want to suspend both of my quarterbacks from a game but I will if I catch you fighting again. Consider this your last warning. Got it?"

We simultaneously answer. "Yes, Coach." But it's a lie and we both know it. This will not be the end of this duel. Henderson won't stop until he gets his spot back.

"You do not speak to each other unless it's required on the field concerning a play. Both of you can think about how to get along while doing ten extra laps after practice."

We return to the field. Henderson goes his way so I proceed in the opposite direction.

"Just couldn't resist, could you?" Dane laughs.

I've never been able to resist a challenge. "Nope."

Dane gestures toward Claire. "Well, it looks like someone has already run out there to tell her what you said judging by the look on her face. I hope she lets you have it good. You deserve whatever she dishes and I hope I'm around to see it when she does. I need a good laugh."

"Wow. Some friend you turned out to be."

"When you deserve support, I'll defend you. But I can't go along with what you just did to Claire."

Damn. I feel like total shit now.

COACH WORKED us hard in practice, and now these extra laps are going to hurt. It ends up working out for the best, though. The cheerleaders finish practice and leave the field while I'm running and I'm glad. I don't want to face Claire's wrath in front of the guys or the cheerleading squad. I guess that sort of makes me a coward, but Dane is right. I've got it coming to me. I'm going to catch hell but it won't be until tomorrow. I have all night to dread it.

Running finished, I head to my truck and see East Franklin's perfect couple standing in the parking lot next to Henderson's fancy-ass car. Coach is there as well. I figure it's a preventive measure on his part. I can't say anything to dickhead but I can't resist taking the opportunity to twist the knife a little by taunting his girl. "You looked good in cheer practice today."

I don't get a response from her but Forbes is livid. I love it. I decide to push the envelope a little further. "See you tomorrow, Claire."

I can't stop this game of getting to Forbes through his girlfriend. It's too damn easy and it's not like it's hurting her. Not really. At the end of the day, it's all innocent. I think.

I DIDN'T SLEEP. Rita got in my face about not selling the dope. She threatened to throw me out, as usual, but that isn't the basis behind my concern. I worried about Claire all night, but not her wrath. I begin to feel like the asshole she accuses me of being.

I get to humanities and she isn't in class yet. I take the same seat as the yesterday and wait. When she enters the classroom, my heart falls to my stomach as I realize I'm less prepared to see her than I thought. I'm uneasy as I gather my words for an apology but she skips the seat next to me and asks Brad to swap places with her, making him my partner for the day.

She's ignoring me, acting as though I'm not even in the room. And I don't like it. Oh, it's a brilliant plan on her part if she wants to get under my skin—it's absolutely working.

Humanities is brutal with Brad as my partner. He chose "recognizing patterns" as our ingredient for discussion but the only pattern I see is him talking and me wanting him to shut up. The only good thing about being partners with Brad is that he enjoys talking just to hear his own voice, which means I don't have to. I watch Claire as he rambles, hoping she'll look in my direction so I can wave my white flag. My partnership with Brad can be considered penance for yesterday's bad behavior.

Claire is up and gone when the bell rings, not giving me an opportunity to apologize. I walk to third period with the intention of making her listen to me whether she likes it or not.

I wait until Claire and her talkative bodyguard have gone into U.S. history before I enter. I'm not giving her another opportunity to get away from me.

She and Payton are sitting in the front row with no open seats around them. She appears to not notice when I enter but two can play this game.

I walk over to the student sitting behind her. "I forgot my glasses today and I can't see the board. Would you mind trading your seat for the one two rows over?"

The girl smiles. "No problem. Sometimes I forget my glasses too."

I sit behind Claire, giving me the upper hand, since I'll be able to lean forward to whisper in her ear. She'll be forced to hear me out, so I waste no time getting down to it. "I know what I did was wrong and I'm sorry. Will you please just go ahead and cuss me out or whatever you have planned?"

No response.

Buckley begins lecturing but I'm not ready to let this go. I need some kind of reaction from her.

The teacher turns his back to pull down a map. I lean close to her ear. "You don't have to continue ignoring me. I get it. You're pissed and you have every right to be. I said I was sorry. What else do you want me to do?"

Payton leans over. "You can give it up because she doesn't accept fauxpologies."

That isn't what I'm dishing. This is the real thing—at least as real as it gets for me. "I'm not being fake. This is me being real and I'm truly sorry."

She flips me off over her shoulder.

Payton leans over again and whispers, "Since she's not speaking to you, I'm going to be kind and translate her sign language for you. It means fauxpology not accepted."

"Yeah, thanks."

I think I may have screwed with the wrong princess.

I lean back in my desk, accepting my temporary defeat while planning my next move.

CHAPTER TEN

CLAIRE DEVERAUX

I spent today ignoring Jesse Boone—except when I gave him the finger—and that doesn't count since I didn't verbally address him.

He thought he knew exactly how the whole thing would play out. He expected me to walk into class, let him have it good, and then accept his smooth apology, but he has another thing coming. I'm not letting him off the hook that easily.

I'm surprised at how well ignoring him has worked, yet I'm aware that he'll grow immune to it soon. I need to come up with a contingency plan and there's no one better to ask than Sergeant Spite. "I have a job and only a devious mind such as yours will do."

"Loving it already," she says, rubbing her hands together like a true villain. "What 'cha got for me?"

"I'm not finished with Jesse Boone. I need an idea—something to make him think twice about using me as ammunition against Forbes."

Payton nods in agreement. "Yes! I'd love to help you put him in the penalty box. In fact, I'd rather enjoy it. Let me think it over and I'll have something together by the end of practice today."

Payton is preoccupied with watching the football players instead of concentrating on cheer routines but I don't mention it since I know she's formulating a perfect plan. At one point during practice, Payton elbows me and motions toward Jesse. "He's watching you between every play. His eyes don't leave you even when Gretchen bends over in those ridiculously short shorts to give him a free look."

I resist the urge to look at him. "Good. If he's watching me, then he can see I'm not looking his way."

"Don't worry. He definitely picks up on what you're laying down and he doesn't care for your lack of interest in him at all. The guy doesn't know but he's giving me the ammunition I need to devise the perfect plan."

After practice, Payton drives me home since I'm still carless. "This plot is simple yet cunning. I'm not sure you're up for it because it'll require work."

"Oh, I'm up for it," I reassure her. I'll do whatever it takes to teach this bad boy he can't use me and get away with it.

"Okay. Jesse Boone may have used you as ammo, but Wilma … the boy wants to be your Fred Flintstone so he can make your Bedrock."

I don't speak cartoon. "I'm failing to hear a plan here, oh brilliant evil one."

"You're going to continue to ignore him for a few days and then you'll act like you're coming around and warming up to him. Once he becomes confident in your newfound friendship, you're going to turn it into a flirtationship and tease him a little. After a couple of weeks, he'll believe you're ready to fall madly in bed with him. Just when he thinks he has you where he wants you, you'll break it down for him and tell him his bad ass just got punked."

This plan isn't coming together for me. "How am I going to have a flirtationship with Jesse Boone while I have a boyfriend?"

"A valid point," she says. "The key is to make him believe you're doing it behind Forbes's back."

"I have to trick Jesse and Forbes? Sounds risky."

"Don't worry. Forbes won't find out because I'll have your

back," she reassures. "The beauty of the whole thing is that you are the one in control, not Jesse. You'll make him jump through hoops to be with you on your terms. I guarantee you'll have him eating out of your hand."

Payton can see my indecision but somehow knows the perfect words to push me over the edge. "Don't forget how he humiliated you in front of the entire football team and cheer squad with his crude announcement. He publicly claimed he was doing you behind Forbes's back. He as good as called you a slut."

"You're right. I'd love to wipe that arrogant, cocky grin off his face." Even if it is one of the most handsome faces I've ever seen.

"Give it until Friday, then ease into the warming-up stage of the plan."

I decide it's a good scheme once I get the gist, but there's no guarantee he'll want me to warm up to him. "You know your plan is shit if he doesn't like me, right?"

Payton laughs. "Trust me. He's going to need a boner barrier to hide the tent in his pants when you're finished with him."

I spend the next three days doing a bang-up job of ignoring Jesse, making him crazy. I think. Per Payton's orders, I'm up early this morning so I can make myself sexier for today's activity of warming up to him. Payton is pleased with both my promptness and appearance when she arrives to chauffeur me to school. And I'm excited that I'll finally have my car back this afternoon.

"Yes! You totally nailed the look I was going for." She motions for me to spin. "Do your best to get paired with him in humanities so it looks like you have no control over it."

"Got it." I remember the tortured look on his face when he partnered with Brad. "That won't be a problem."

"I wish I could be with you but I know you'll make me proud."

We pull into the parking lot and Payton is sure to park next to him. He's sitting in his truck smoking a cigarette. "Wish me luck."

I pretend to return to the car for something I've forgotten so

Payton can go ahead of me. I time it perfectly so Jesse and I are walking to the building together. I'm only a few steps ahead. I'm disappointed when we're halfway to the front door and he hasn't said a word. But then he calls out. "Hey, are you going to force me into partnering with one of the brainiacs today?"

I grin but don't answer as I continue walking. "I guess that's a yes?"

I go over the plan in my head as I follow my usual morning routine, feeling confident when I walk into humanities one period later. Jesse looks up and watches me walk toward him. I'm certain he expects me to ask Brad to swap seats as I've done every day this week but today, I sit in the desk next to him.

"Did you decide you were finished ignoring me?" He sounds hopeful.

I busy myself by digging in my backpack to retrieve a binder. I open it to prepare for class, not acknowledging him or his words.

"If you plan to continue giving me the silent treatment, why did you sit there? You can do a much better job at it from across the room." He sighs. "You know you'll have to talk to me if we work in pairs today."

Mrs. Tanner shuts the classroom door and joins us in the circle. "Today we're going to continue discussing our six ingredients for creativity. You may keep your previous partner or choose a new one. The only requirement is that you pick an ingredient neither of you have previously discussed."

I don't make a move to claim another partner, and neither does Jesse. He looks so pleased.

I look at our options on the board. "Which ones do you have left to cover?"

"Oh, she speaketh to me?" He's sarcastic—not really the best way for him to start off with me today.

I don't acknowledge his comment. "You and I completed 'seeing in new ways' on Monday. What did you cover with Brad yesterday?"

"'Recognizing patterns.'"

"Perfect. Kara and I did that one as well. Do you have a preference for today?"

"I think 'challenging assumptions' is fitting. Wouldn't you agree?"

"Fine. It has to be done at some point." I open the assignment envelope provided by Mrs. Tanner and read the directions aloud. "'List three assumptions you've made about your partner and provide the evidence behind the reason why. Once your list is complete, be prepared to either agree with your partner's opinion or persuade his/her belief.'"

"That doesn't seem a whole lot different than the preconceived notions activity on Monday."

This could get deep but it's actually perfect if I play my cards right. "This time you must show the evidence behind your assumption, rather than accept it simply as opinion."

He looks worried. "Hmm … I may find out exactly how little you think of me. I hope I don't get my feelings hurt too badly."

I don't respond as I open my composition book to begin listing my assumptions and the evidence supporting them. I'm still working on the second one when Jesse finishes. I don't dare look up but I can feel his stare. "If you don't stop ogling me, I'm going to make the assumption that you are creepy."

He laughs. "You haven't even looked in my direction so why would you think that?"

"I feel your eyes on me."

"No one can feel eyes on them." I notice he doesn't deny that he was staring.

"I'm finished. Let's do this. I'll even go first." I lift my comp book and clear my throat. "You smoke cigarettes so I assume you do not care about your health." Hah! I'd like to see him argue that one.

He leans back in his desk and crosses his arms. "I smoke but that doesn't mean I don't care about my health. I was young when I started. I didn't understand the risks associated with it but now that I'm older, I want to quit. Unfortunately, it isn't the easiest thing in the world to do."

"So, you're too weak to quit?"

That gets his full attention. "Addicted to nicotine? Yes. But weak? No. Never mistake me for weak, princess."

Jesse Boone doesn't have to convince me how strong he is. I hear his strength when he speaks. I see it in his eyes and recognize it in his persistence when he refused to give up on talking to me this week while I ignored him.

"You're next. Enlighten me about … me," I say.

He grins. In the short time I've known him, I've learned that there is always mischief behind those dimples. "I hear that your parents are friends with the Hendersons. Considering that Forbes is a complete dick, I assume you date him because it pleases your parents and it's not really what you want."

How can a school assignment get so personal, so quickly? "Please, don't be afraid to get personal about things that are none of your business."

"The exercise doesn't say anything about avoiding personal issues, so spill. Are you madly in love with Forbes or are you sleeping with him until someone better comes along?"

I can't believe he just asked that. "You're a total jackass."

"I've been called worse but you're avoiding the question, princess."

I don't know if I want him to think I'm sleeping with Forbes or not. "He's my boyfriend. That's all you need to know."

He smirks. "You aren't in love with him."

He's right. I don't love Forbes but it's not a discussion I want to have with Jesse Boone. "I didn't say that."

"Yes, you did."

I pick up my paper and rip it down the middle. "Okay. Two can play this game."

He sits straighter in his desk, appearing more interested. "Do your worst, princess."

Do I dare to make this assignment a battle in the war I've declared against him? Yes, I think I do. "You act like you don't give a shit about anything in the world but you didn't want me to be mad at you."

"What's the evidence to back your assumption?"

"You tried to apologize the moment you saw me. I can refresh your memory if you don't remember." I puff up my chest and begin mocking him. "'I'm not being fake. This is me being real and I'm truly sorry.'"

He looks down at his paper and I laugh at how easily I wipe that cocky grin from his face.

"I apologized because what I did was wrong and I felt bad about it. You're acting like that makes me a wuss."

I've clearly touched a nerve. "I didn't say you were a wuss. It's actually sort of the opposite."

"What does that mean?"

"You've spent the whole week trying to get me to forgive you for what you said." And here goes me stepping out on to a limb. "You care what I think of you."

"It sounds like you put a lot of thought into that—more than what you could have in the last fifteen minutes—so I assume you've been thinking about me."

He has no idea how right he is. I think about him way more than I should but I would die before I admitted it. "Only because thinking about you was part of the assignment."

"You're lying. It's all over your blushing face."

I'm sick and tired of everyone reading my face. "It's red because you make my blood boil."

"You blood is boiling because you're hot for me. That's why you feel like you're on fire."

Oh God. My cheeks are pulsating.

None of this is part of the plan. I'm supposed to be the one in control.

I contemplate what to say next and I'm saved by the bell. Literally. I gather my things and then glance in his direction. Smug arrogance spreads across his face and my inner beotch steps forward to take control. I refuse to let him win this round.

I wait outside the exit and motion with a single finger for him to come to me.

"Have something to admit, princess?"

Easing into the warming-up stage is no longer an option. What I'm about to do would be considered more like jumping in head first. "You fictitiously announced that I liked what your hands did to me but I'm the one who just made you come with one finger. Tell me now who has the skills." I give him a wink and a moment for it to sink in before I walk away.

I hear him call out behind me, "Is this the game we're going to play, princess? Because if it is, you should know I don't back down from a challenge."

I never feared he would. Panic sets in and I'm certainly concerned about what I've gotten myself into.

CHAPTER ELEVEN

JESSE BOONE

I LIKE THIS VERSION OF THE PRINCESS. SHE'S FUN AND RECEPTIVE TO PLAY.

Although I like this change in Claire, I'm not prepared for it. I need time to strategize. I avoid sitting next to her in third period history by planting myself in a desk on the other side of the room. I do it so she doesn't distract me, but I can't stop my eyes from wandering in her direction.

She doesn't look my way but her conversation with Payton appears to be deep. Why do I get the feeling they're plotting?

I don't think Claire has the ability to cause too much damage but I'm not so sure about Payton. I think that one could be a wildcat.

I hurry to physics, hoping to see Claire without Forbes so we can have a moment to play. She walks through the door alone and I'm pleased. I swivel in her direction and realize too late I must look like a grinning hyena.

"What's with the shit-eating grin?"

Damn. I've given myself away without saying a word. "I was just thinking … you might as well sleep with me since everyone already thinks you have. I promise you won't be disappointed. Money-back guarantee."

She shakes her head and laughs. "You're reality challenged. No one believes we're sleeping together."

"I've decided I'm interested in finding out what your whole hand can do since you were able to make me come with one finger."

"If this is the real you, then whoever told you to be yourself couldn't have given you worse advice."

She didn't tell me to go to hell, so that's promising. "Go out with me tonight. It's our last free Friday night for months. I promise to rock your world."

"You know I have a boyfriend, so why are you even asking?"

I place my open palm over my heart. "Because I'm a hopeless romantic." She looks toward the door and then back to me. "He doesn't have to know. I'm very good at keeping secrets."

Her eyes grow large and she gestures toward the dick walking in. "I can't."

"Someday you'll call me the one that got away." Let her think on that for the next hour.

I face the front of the classroom and hear Henderson sit behind me. "Hey, babe. Having a good day?"

"Yeah. It's been a really good one so far—very interesting. I found out that I really like something I once believed I didn't care for at all." She's referring to me. I know she is.

"I hope you find some other things you like tonight."

Sounds like she has plans with her boyfriend. It's Friday night, so why wouldn't she? And why do I feel so jilted?

Gretchen comes in looking especially slutty in a short skirt and low-cut shirt. She immediately focuses her attention on me—as she has every day this week—so I decide to return her friendliness in an attempt to bait Claire.

I make a show of looking her up and down and raise my voice so my words will easily reach Claire's ears. "Damn, Gretchen! You look smoking-hot today. That shirt looks great on you." I stare at her cleavage. "It accents your ... eyes."

She grins like the cat that ate the canary and leans closer to stroke my arm. "Thank you very much. I'm glad to know you're finally paying attention."

"Don't think I haven't been noticing." How could I not when she shoves her tits in my face every day?

I hear the slam of a binder against the table behind me. "What's up with you?" Forbes says.

"Absolutely nothing," Claire answers.

Trifling with Gretchen is getting Claire's attention, so I want to test my theory by taking flirting a step further. "You got plans for tonight?"

Gretchen leans closer, giving me a bird's-eye view of her cleavage. "I do, but nothing that can't include you. I'm supposed to go to a bonfire at Harrison Cleveland's. Half the school will be there—the cool half, that is. His older brother is buying some kegs. I told Ben Averitt I would go with him, but I can bail on him if you want to be my date."

I stare at her tits to make her—and Claire—think I'm interested. "I think you would have a better time with me. Don't you agree?"

"Completely."

There's another loud slam behind us. This time it's a textbook onto the floor, causing Gretchen to jump. She twists in her seat and shoots daggers at Claire. "Clumsy much?"

Claire returns the glare. "Slutty much?"

"News flash, Claire. A chastity belt is not a fashion statement," Gretchen scoffs.

Claire narrows her eyes. "At least my right leg doesn't miss my left because they haven't seen each other in so long."

"Contrary to what you may believe, being a prude is not a virtue."

"Gretchen, the smartest thing to ever come out of your mouth is a guy's dick."

"Whoooa, Claire!" Henderson says.

The girls quiet down as Mrs. Bishop starts her lecture, but I can't stop analyzing the motive behind Claire's verbal attack. Does she dislike Gretchen that much, or is she jealous? I hope it's the latter.

Claire is the first one out the door when class ends, Henderson close behind her. With her absence, I'm left with little reason to talk to Gretchen but she wants to iron out details. "What time do you want to pick me up?"

I'm not getting stuck with this slut all night. "I have somewhere to be early Saturday morning so I'll be leaving the bonfire early. It's best if we meet there."

She cozies up to me, letting her tits brush my arm. "I'm all right with leaving the party early."

I know what kind of bait that is but I'm not biting. "I might have to leave really early and I wouldn't want to ruin your good time."

She frowns when I don't budge. "Okay, I guess that'll work."

She gives me directions to Harrison's and says to meet her there at eight. I agree but I'm still up in the air if I'll show since her intentions are clear. She isn't planning a reunion between her left and right leg tonight and I'm not interested in a girl who has seen more ceilings than Michelangelo.

Is the mess I've gotten myself into with Gretchen worth the attempt to bring out Claire's green-eyed monster?

I run into Dane in the hall and we bump fists. "Hey, Boone. You coming to Harrison's bonfire tonight?"

"I'm supposed to go with Gretchen but I'm not sure I'm going to make it."

"You should come. Harrison says there's going to be plenty of beer."

I wonder what her response would be if I stood her up. "I'm guessing Gretchen will be pissed if I don't show since I asked her to ditch Ben."

"Well, at least I won't have to worry about you messing with Claire to make Forbes mad. You'll have your hands too full of Gretchen's tits for that nonsense."

Game changer. If the princess is going, then I am too. "Are you sure Claire will be there?"

"Yeah. We're using her car for the music since she has a custom sound system."

I'm really questioning if Claire is the girl I think she is. "I changed my mind. I'm definitely going."

"Do I dare ask who the persuading factor is?" Dane says.

"I'm fairly certain you can guess but I'll give you one clue: it's not the girl with more pricks than a secondhand dartboard."

"Would it do any good to ask you to not start anything with Forbes?"

My focus is becoming less and less about that asshole. "I don't have the intention of fighting Forbes but if me and Claire decide we want to talk, then no one is going to stop us."

"I'm assuming she's accepted your apology if you think she might talk to you."

"I believe she has but only after she's made sure I got what was coming to me." That old saying is true. Hell hath no fury like a woman scorned. "I'm not sure she's finished with me yet, but I damn sure want to find out."

"Please, be careful. Forbes and his posse are still gunning for you, and there's only a week left until the first game. Don't do anything to push the envelope tonight," Dane warns.

"I've told you I'm not afraid of them." I almost want to tell Dane about the things I've lived through so he'll lay off.

"And I've told you Forbes doesn't play by the rules, so I guess we'll have to agree to disagree."

An impasse it is. "I guess so."

CHAPTER TWELVE

CLAIRE DEVERAUX

W‍HAT'S WRONG WITH ME? I ACTED LIKE A COMPLETE IMBECILE WHEN JESSE gave the sexual butterfly a little bit of attention. Okay. It wasn't just attention. It was more like … foreplay.

The worst part of my whole display isn't that I'm afraid Forbes will see right through me. It's that I'm afraid Jesse won't.

The rush I felt while talking with him today confirms the intense, undeniable attraction I have for him. This is a problem for more than one reason.

Although I'm playing a game, I thought he shared the same attraction. He seemed to be so into me but then he asked that whore out on a date and as good as rubbed my nose in it.

The boundaries of this scam are becoming increasingly unclear. The idea of Gretchen using Jesse as her next screwvenir makes me crazy, but the thought of him saying yes to her nauseates me. This is an even bigger problem. I don't want him to want Gretchen because … I want him to want me instead.

Oh, shit.

This whole thing is whack. I have a boyfriend and not just any boyfriend—a long-term one my parents basically handpicked.

Forbes Henderson is everything they want for me.

What do I really even know about Jesse Boone? He's from Collinsville—a good indicator that he's probably poorer than a church mouse. If his prior zip code doesn't prove it, then his truck certainly does. I bet he'll be the first person in his family to graduate from high school.

And he's a smoker! How in the world could I be attracted to someone with such a nasty habit? It's so skanky, yet something about the way he holds a cigarette between his thumb and index finger is incredibly sexy. I love the way he brings it to the corner of his full lips for a drag. Mmm … another rebel without a cause.

I wish he smelled like stale smoke. At least I could find that unappealing. But he doesn't. His fragrance is clean, woodsy, and masculine. It's intoxicating, inviting me to come closer.

It'll be Gretchen enjoying the way he smells tonight, not me. I'm sure she'll be wearing his aroma before the night ends.

Fourth period drags. I spend the whole time thinking about Jesse and how he'll spend the evening with that whore. I torture myself with the same thoughts during the next period so I'm a total mess by the time school's over.

I want to rush Payton along so Forbes doesn't see me like this. Or Jesse. "Payton, I really need to get going."

"Okay. Do you still need me to drop you to pick up your car?"

"Yeah, we're using it tonight at the bonfire for the music."

"Love it," she sings. "That means we get to pick the tunes."

Like a bad nightmare, we run into Jesse on the way to Payton's car. Great—just what I didn't need. "Hey, Claire, will I see you at the bonfire?" He's smirking, almost as if he knows how anxious I'm feeling.

I should say something nonchalant and walk away but I don't. "Well, I guess that all depends."

"On what?"

"If you spend the whole night screwing Gretchen, then I'd guess not." I sound rude, possibly even bordering on possessive. I should've kept my mouth shut.

"Have I done something to upset you, Claire?" Shit. I can't look at him but I'm sure he's smirking—laughing at my obvious display of jealousy.

I sigh. "No, Jesse. You haven't done anything to upset me." We aren't in a relationship so he can be with whomever he chooses.

"Good. Maybe I'll see you later if I decide against screwing Gretchen all night."

I can't speak for fear I might vomit. He's antagonizing me and we both know it. He must realize the effects of his words—why else would he be so bold?

Payton and I get into her car, parked right next to his. "Wow. He really wants to hear you tell him to ditch Gretchen."

She's so obsessed with the plan that she fails to see the effect he has on me. That's probably best.

I look at him sitting in his truck. He's watching me—maybe even waiting to see if I'll get out of Payton's car and come to him. He could be hoping I'd beat my hand on the glass and scream at him to not be with her tonight. Maybe all I have to do is say the words and he'll dump Gretchen.

I place my hand on the handle but hesitate as my heart beats out of my chest. If I go to him now, I'm a goner for sure. It won't have a thing to do with strategical thinking and then Payton will figure it all out.

I close my eyes because I don't want to look at him anymore. "Just go."

"You're blowing the plan, Claire. What is wrong with you?"

I open my eyes and stare forward. "I just need you to get me out of here. Now."

I'm sure Payton can't make heads nor tails of my actions but I play it off as though I got nervous about the plan. It's my only chance at saving myself from being busted by the human lie detector.

My afternoon is marginally better because I finally get my car back.

That means it's my turn to drive, so I pick Payton up and head toward Harrison's. I listen as she explains the updated version of our plan to take down Jesse.

"He plans on getting laid tonight if he's coming to the bonfire with Gretchen. There's no other reason for a male to have contact with that walking mattress, but we can't let it happen. His attention must be on you."

"How am I going to accomplish that?"

"Tell him you're into him but you're afraid. You've invested a lot in your relationship with Forbes and you need time to think. The cock block comes into play when you tell him that he can forget about anything between the two of you if he touches that slut. Insist that you will never do the penivore's leftovers."

Damn, this girl is good but there could be one flaw. "What if I don't see him before he gets with Gretchen? That slut puppy is fast."

"We're getting there first since we're in charge of music. Your job will be to make sure you get him away from the crowd to talk before she has a chance to drop her panties."

I can't be in two places at once. "I don't mean to insult your skills of deception but are you going to be able to keep Forbes occupied while I talk to him?"

"Not a problem. The funnel will do the job for us. He'll down a few beers and time will no longer exist. You'll be free the rest of the night."

Payton with a beer funnel and a crowd of guys is dangerous business. She has a way of getting them to do anything she wants. "I don't need you to kill them with alcohol poisoning. Just keep Forbes and his buddies busy for a little while."

"I can't be charged with anything if he does it himself. Either way, you're covered."

"Thanks." I think.

The beer's flowing, the fire's burning, and the music's bumping. But there's no sign of Jesse and Gretchen. "Relax, chick. It's still early. They won't get here until a little later, so you've got plenty of time."

"Got time for what?" Forbes asks as he comes up from behind to wrap his arms around my waist. He lowers his mouth to kiss my neck and I'm able to admit to myself for the first time that I feel absolutely nothing when he touches me. If I'm being honest with myself, I never have. I can't recall a moment when I longed to be with him. That alone tells me everything I need to know about our relationship.

Harrison's brother comes through with the kegs as promised and I don't know who is more pleased by the presence of alcohol—me or Forbes and his pals.

Forbes passes me a red plastic cup filled with beer. "Let's get this party started."

"You don't think it's a little early to begin drinking? We'll be wasted before nine if we start now."

His brow rises. "Precisely."

I take the beer and gulp because I need to calm my nerves before Jesse gets here. I don't want to freak out the way I did earlier.

Forbes's eyes light up like he's hit the jackpot. "Now, that's what I'm talking about. Check out my girl, Coop. I told you she wasn't a princess."

My heart feels like it jumps into my throat. "Why did you call me that?"

"I didn't call you anything. I said you weren't a princess. What's the big deal if I did?" He takes a long guzzle, and I'm relieved when I realize the use of Jesse's nickname for me is only a coincidence.

"Nothing. Forget I said anything."

"You're being weird tonight. Does that mean you're nervous about something?" He's hopeful tonight will be the night he gets what he wants from me. Wrong.

I'm incredibly nervous but it has nothing to do with him.

I'm no fool. I know pushing beer on me is a ploy to loosen my panties.

Jesse coming along hasn't altered my feelings toward Forbes because there has never been love in my heart for him. He's a safe choice, one that meets everyone's expectations for me. But I no longer want to live for what my family and friends expect from me. Tonight I do what makes me happy.

CHAPTER THIRTEEN

JESSE BOONE

Damn. Talk about a total letdown. For a minute, I thought I had Claire ready to jump out of that car to tell me to ditch Gretchen. She looked so close.

Claire needs a gentle push in the right direction—or maybe a hard shove—and I'm prepared to give her that. It's probably wrong to use Gretchen in the process but something tells me this won't be the first time she's been used and cast aside. Something tells me she doesn't mind. Maybe it's sort of her thing.

I arrive at eight, but not because I want to be prompt for Gretchen. I need plenty of time with Claire to show her what she's missing by not being with me.

I wince a little when I figure out that the luxury convertible parked in the middle of the field pumping music belongs to Claire. Man, being confident was easier when I didn't know she had a car worth more than the trailer I live in.

I put away thoughts of material things and remind myself how she reacted when I flirted with Gretchen. She seemed so close to giving in.

I get out of my truck and drop the tailgate. I sit, scanning the field for the princess, and Dane comes over to join me. "Glad to see you made it. Where's your lady friend?"

I assume he's referring to Gretchen. I'm not sure you can call that one a lady. "I haven't seen her yet." I scour the field again in search of the princess. "I'm not looking forward to finding her. It's not going to go well when she figures out we don't have the same agenda."

"What exactly is your plan for tonight?"

"Things with Claire have changed since we talked."

"How so?" he asks.

"I ran into her after school and we had an interesting interaction." I can't stop smiling as I recall the whole thing. "I think I almost had her."

"You almost had her? What does that mean?"

She was definitely unhappy about my plans. "I think she was close to telling me to ditch Gretchen tonight."

He looks skeptical. "I think you're wrong about that."

He didn't see her face or how troubled she looked. "You weren't there."

"Dude, I hate to break it to you but Forbes says tonight is the night for him and Claire."

That can only mean one thing in a guy's book. "What is that supposed to mean?"

"He says he's tapping it tonight." Dane laughs but I find nothing humorous.

"I assume you mean Claire and not a keg." If he's bragging about tapping it tonight, then that means it'll be a first. Good to know.

I like knowing she hasn't given herself to him. No. Delight is probably a better word and this newfound knowledge makes me think I don't have Claire Deveraux figured out at all.

"I wish you the best of luck if Claire is into you, but be prepared for Henderson's wrath. It won't be pretty if you take his girl, especially if he thinks he's finally getting what he's worked on for so long."

I search the field again and finally see Claire through the bonfire's golden flames. She's standing with a small group—next to Forbes and Payton. "I'd be disappointed if his wrath was anything less than ugly."

Our eyes meet and we simultaneously smile but hers fades quickly as a hand touches my arm. Ugh, my date has arrived.

Dane takes Gretchen's arrival as his cue to leave. "I'll catch up with you guys later."

My plan to arrive before Gretchen so I could talk to Claire is blown to smithereens.

"Been here long?" she asks as she sits on the tailgate.

"Nah. About five minutes."

She looks around for a minute. "You wanna go for a ride?"

Wow. She wastes no time but I don't know why I'm surprised. The girl has a turbocharged sex drive. "I'm good. Let's just hang out here for a while." This chick needs a distraction. "You want a beer?"

"Sure." Her voice is drenched with disappointment. I hope she doesn't pout. I hate when they do that.

Maybe she'll get drunk and pass out so I can talk to Claire without her bugging me. "I'll grab us a couple. Be right back."

I'm filling a cup for my date when Claire comes over. She stands behind me, waiting in line for a refill. "Thirsty, princess?"

"Yeah. I'll let you fill me up." She bites her lower lip, grinning as she waits for my response.

Nope. That didn't come out wrong. It sounded just as she intended. "You have everyone fooled, don't you?"

She laughs. "Not everyone, I'm afraid."

I shake my head. "No. You don't have me fooled in the least."

"People who've known me my entire life can't see who I really am ... but you can. How is that possible?"

She puts on a front and I do too. I've done it most of my life—pretending everything is okay. "Maybe we're more alike than you know."

She looks around and steps closer. "I need to talk to you—alone—but I can't right now."

There they are—the words I've been dying to hear. "What do you have in mind?"

"Give me at least half an hour and then meet me in those woods." She points toward an area. "Right over there."

"Okay."

I return with Gretchen's beer and she begins her interrogation. "What did Miss Goody-Goody have to say to you?"

"Nothing you'd care to hear," I reply dryly.

"I'm certain of that but was it anything you cared to hear?"

We're not having this conversation. "Don't go there."

"The virgin queen with a boyfriend acts mad as hell the minute you give me some attention and now she's talking to you when her boyfriend isn't looking. Something is going on between the two of you." She needs to let this go.

I lift my plastic cup to take a drink of beer, avoiding eye contact.

"You aren't denying it."

I think on it a second before deciding I need a smoke. "I'm not afflicted with the need to explain myself to anyone." My tone is harsh, a warning for her to drop it.

"Geez, no need to get pissed off about it." She reaches over and takes the cigarette and lighter from my hand. She brings it to her lips and fires it up before taking a long drag. "I don't give a rat's ass if you're after each other. I'm only interested in figuring out if I need to find another date because mine is fixated on someone besides me."

"Do you want to hear me say I'm fixated on you or would you rather hear the truth?"

She looks angry. "You bastard. You knew all along you were going to try to get with her. That's why you wouldn't pick me up."

Winner, winner. Chicken dinner. The girl may not be so dense after all, but I'm not ready to admit anything except maybe that I'm not into her. "I didn't want to get stuck with you all night. It has nothing to do with Claire."

She looks unconvinced. "You used me to make Claire Deveraux jealous—and it worked. I'd be pissed if I wasn't feeling so gratified."

She really dislikes Claire. "Glad we both get something we want out of this."

"I haven't gotten what I want by a long shot." She takes another drag and I see that I won't be getting that cigarette back. "You didn't have to trick me into making her jealous. I would've gladly done it for fun but now that I know what's going on, I'll gladly help you any way you'd like."

"I think I'm good for now." I barely get the refusal out when she leans over and possesses my mouth with hers.

Oh hell.

She pulls away and looks at Claire, gloating. "Sorry. I couldn't resist."

Bullshit. She's not sorry in the least.

Thirty minutes passes and Claire doesn't leave her spot by Forbes's side. I see him holding her hand and occasionally placing kisses on her neck. I don't care at all for the feeling it stirs in me.

I remain on the tailgate of my truck talking with Gretchen but I'm constantly looking over at what appears to be a happy couple. Has she changed her mind about sneaking away into the woods because of Gretchen's kiss?

It's almost an hour later when I see her sneak away from a very drunk Forbes. I wait a moment before walking in her direction so no one will suspect anything.

"Psst ... over here." I find the princess peeking out from behind a tree. I go to her and she abandons her hiding place to come around and lean against the tree.

"Hey, princess." I no longer say the nickname to patronize her. I'm using it in an entirely different way.

"You managed to get away from the penivore."

I'm confused. "The what?"

"You know. Herbivore. Carnivore. Gretchen is better known as a penivore."

Oh. She gives blow jobs. "I would've asked her out sooner if I'd known that."

Claire makes a fist and hits me as hard as she can in the chest before walking away. I rub the dull ache and use my free hand to grab her arm. "I'm kidding, princess."

She yanks free but I stop her from fleeing by stepping in front of her. We're chest to chest, eye to eye, and she backs away until her back is flush with the tree again.

I advance on Claire. She looks breathless, her chest heaving rapidly. "There's something you want to talk about?"

"Yes," she whispers.

"I'm listening." I wait with hopeful anticipation. I want to hear her say she's interested in me.

She's silent so I lean forward and place my lips close to her ear. "Why do you look so frightened? I promise I won't bite … unless you ask me to," I whisper.

She turns her face toward mine and the softness of her cheek grazes my stubbled face. She skims her lips along my jawline until the warmth of her breath hovers at my mouth. We're as close as two people can be without touching. It's torture. I think I'll spontaneously combust if I don't feel her lips on mine.

"I want to kiss you, but I shouldn't," she murmurs against my mouth.

"I want to kiss you—and I don't have a reason not to—but I won't until you ask me to." I'm giving the control to her because I don't trust myself to not scare her away. "What did you want to talk about?"

"I wanted to ask if there was something happening between us." Her eyes search mine. "But I think I have my answer."

"My attraction to you is clear." I rub my thumb over her bottom lip. "Do you really think you have to ask?"

Geez, her lips are so soft when they move against my finger. "I have to be positive because I need to ask you something."

I'm excited to hear what she wants. "The anticipation is killing me."

"I have an intense attraction to you." She stops, I think waiting for a response.

"I feel the same." I silently plead for her to go on.

"But I have an issue." Uh-oh. I don't like the sound of that. "It's Forbes. I think I'm ready to end things but I've invested a year and a half of my life with him. I need to be certain."

I have to convince her to dump him. "What can I do to help you be sure?"

"I need time to feel things out. Are you willing to give that to me?"

Does she mean what I think she means? "You want to sneak around behind his back?"

She scrunches her nose—and she should—because what she's proposing stinks. "I know it's not ideal but I need to know it's the right decision."

This isn't what I'd originally planned but screwing around behind Forbes's back could sweeten the whole thing. "How much time are we talking about?"

"I don't know. I've never done anything like this before. A week—maybe two, tops. And there's something else I need that you might not find so reasonable."

I graze my nose up the side of her neck. "Tell me what else you want from me."

"Ditch Gretchen," she squeaks. "If you sleep with her, there's no chance for us. I don't do her leftovers."

That won't be a problem but I'm not telling her that.

I remember what Dane told me about Forbes's plan for Claire tonight and I think it's only fair the same rules apply to her.

I lean away so I can see her face. "I'll agree to not sleep with Gretchen if you do the same."

"Not a problem. There's no way I'd sleep with that whore."

Hmm, she's a funny girl too? "You know what I mean. You can't screw Forbes if I can't screw Gretchen."

She reaches out and touches my chest, sending my pulse racing. "I agree if you do."

Not only am I cock blocking Forbes, I have his girlfriend thinking of me while she's with him. I couldn't be happier.

"Agreed."

She looks over her shoulder and sighs. "I should get back before they miss me."

If my time with Claire is over, I'm outta here. "I think I'll go."

"Why so early?" Does she really need to ask?

"I may have agreed to sneak around with you but I don't want to watch you hang out with your boyfriend. There's no point in staying if we can't spend time together."

She looks disappointed. "Then I guess I won't see you again until class on Monday. Want to be my partner? We still need to cover 'making connections.'"

"I think we just mastered that one."

CHAPTER FOURTEEN

CLAIRE DEVERAUX

FORBES AND HIS FRIENDS ARE COMPLETELY WASTED. PAYTON PULLS ME ASIDE TO question me about my secret rendezvous in the woods. "How'd it go? I was right, wasn't I? He wants you." She's so sure of herself.

I recall how near Jesse and I were and chills radiate down my body. "His face was so close to mine I could feel the warmth of his breath on my mouth. But he didn't kiss me and said he wouldn't until I asked him to. What kind of game is he playing?"

"No game. He wants you on his terms because he doesn't see that you're the one in control." She shoves my shoulder. "Why didn't you ask him to kiss you, dummy?"

"I don't know." I shrug. "Maybe because asking a guy to kiss me when my boyfriend is standing fifty yards away is a little hinky."

"Yeah," she agrees. "That could qualify as sketchy, even if it's for the sake of the plan."

"Ya think?"

"I probably would've done it."

"Yes, I'm sure you would have."

I look at Jesse getting into his truck and then back to Forbes's drunk ass acting like a buffoon. There isn't enough tolerance juice in those kegs for me to stay and deal with a wasted, horny Forbes the rest of the night. I have about thirty seconds before the only interesting thing here leaves in an old, junked-out truck, so I make a snap decision without any thought for consequences.

"Forbes and Cooper are trashed and I don't feel like babysitting. Do you think you could cover for me and get my car home safely?"

"Sure, but it might be in the morning, depending on how things go."

I hug her. "No problem. Thanks a bunch. You're a sweetheart."

She's steadily talking as I'm leaving. "If your car is staying here, how are you getting home? And what am I supposed to tell Forbes?"

I turn and walk backward. "I'm gonna catch a ride with Jesse so I can work on the plan. You know ... strike while the iron is hot. Just make something up to tell Forbes. He's too trashed to know the difference and you can text me later so we can get our stories straight."

I hear the roar of Jesse's pickup coming to life. I have to hurry. "I'll call you tomorrow and tell you everything."

I start running when the truck pulls forward but I catch up, knocking on the driver's side window so he lowers it. "Is something wrong?"

"Everything's fine but I was hoping to catch a ride with you. I mean ... if I'm not too far out of your way."

"Sure. No problem."

I start around to the passenger side of the truck but he stops me. "Wait."

He gets out, coming around to open the door. Wow. Forbes has never done that.

I quickly climb in, hoping to not be seen. My heart races, my stomach flutters. I'm simultaneously nervous and excited about where my risky move will take me tonight.

He's so different from Forbes and the others. No khaki twills or pastel polos for this guy. He's wearing stonewashed jeans and a fitted black T-shirt embellished with scrolling designs. It's very much like the tattoo on his arm.

He gets back in and the door screeches as he pulls it closed. "Sorry. I've been meaning to take care of that." He puts the truck in drive and pulls away, leaving the only world I know behind. Being with him tonight is going to change everything.

He stops where the edge of the property meets the road. "Which way are we going?"

I don't have a clue. The only thing I know for sure is that I'm not ready for him to take me to my house. "Are you in a rush to get home?"

He laughs. "No. What about you?"

"My parents won't be expecting me anytime soon."

He looks both directions. "Which way do you want to go?"

Why do I feel like his question is putting me at a crossroads? "Surprise me."

"Don't say that unless you mean it." I think it's a warning.

"I mean it. Take me wherever you want."

I can barely see his handsome face illuminated by the dim dashboard lights but a smile spreads. It's not the mischievous grin I usually see. "Okay. I'm going to surprise you but don't forget you asked for it."

He pulls out onto the road and my heart is beating so hard, I can hear it pounding in my ears. The more I concentrate on it, the more nervous I become. I reach for the radio, hoping some music might distract from it. I see two knobs and several buttons but I have no idea how to work them. The thing is ancient.

I retract my hand. "Do you mind turning on some music?"

He twists the knob on the left. "Sure. You can choose the station."

"I've never seen a radio like this."

"It's original to the truck but it still works." He points to the knob on the right. "Twist this one to tune in the station."

The first song I find is a new release by a country band on the pop charts. A crossover, they call it.

"Country music fan?" he quizzes.

"Not at all but I like this song. It's sweet." I shrug, although he can't see me while he's driving. "It's about the kind of love everyone wants to find." What a weird thing to say. I think the beer I drank has my tongue a little too loose.

"I'm not into country music, either, but I like this song too."

"Where are we going?"

"It's a surprise, remember?"

"Oh yeah. Sorry. I forgot." I don't know why but I strongly suspect he's taking me to Collinsville.

It's a fifteen-minute drive to our destination. We talk nonstop on the way, and although Jesse avoids sharing anything personal, I can tell he's taking me somewhere special. "I have two places I want to show you. This is the first."

I look around and see a playground, picnic tables, and a lake. "A park?"

"Yeah."

I reach for the lever on the door but he stops me. "No. Let me." He performs the same routine as earlier and I step out. "You're a princess so you deserve to be treated as such."

I get out and he shuts my door. "You can be pretty unassholeish at times so I should probably find a new name for you."

"I'm all for that but you're not getting a new one. I could never think of you as anything else but princess." That name once pissed me off, but I've come to love it when it comes out of his mouth.

He takes my hand and his touch ignites an excitement in me— something I've never felt with Forbes.

He leads me toward a large play area. "Do you see a common theme?" I don't answer so he prompts me. "Perhaps something fit for a princess." He uses his hand to point out a specific section, narrowing my search. "It may be difficult to see since it's dark but look in this area and see if anything registers with you."

I study the playset he has pointed out and it suddenly hits me. "It's a castle."

"Princess Claire," he laughs. "Welcome to my Collinsville kingdom."

I don't know if it's the beer or something else but I feel playful. "Will you give me the royal tour?"

"Absolutely."

We climb the child-size drawbridge and sit inside the wooden castle. "This was my kingdom when I was growing up." He points to the corner. "Over there's where I had my first kiss."

"What's her name so I'll know who to be jealous of?"

He shrugs. "I never caught her name but she was a cute blond."

I cross my arms, pretending to be miffed. "So you prefer blonds? I see how you are."

"There were no cute little auburn-haired girls running around or I'm sure I would've chosen differently," he jokes. "I was only eight, so what did I know? I started smoking when I was twelve so I think we've already established that I wasn't the brightest kid."

We hang out in the castle talking—until I lose my buzz—but he still reveals no personal details.

"This has been fun, but there's somewhere else I'd like to take you."

"Sure." I'll gladly go anywhere he wants. I enjoy his company.

We leave the park and he drives a few minutes until we are in an open field, parked in the middle.

He leaves the key in the ignition so the radio will continue playing. "I'm sure you're wondering why we're in the middle of this field."

"Sort of … since there's nothing here."

He touches a finger to his temple. "It's all right here. You just can't see it because it's in my head."

He reaches across the cab and takes my hand to pull me across the bench seat toward him. I'm positive he's going to kiss me—and I'll let him—but then he doesn't. Instead, he opens his door and steps out.

I'm puzzled by this but I remember what he said. He won't kiss me until I ask him to.

"This place is significant to me. It's where I learned to play football." It doesn't look like anything more than an open field in need of mowing but I see the seriousness when he tells me it's important. "This was Collinsville's football field when I was a kid. I spent half my life right here learning how to throw a football."

"Looks like the practice paid off, Mister Starting Quarterback."

I sit in the driver's seat facing Jesse while he props against the open door. "I hope. Football is important for me. It isn't a pastime or a popularity contest. Since it seems you've stolen my chance at being valedictorian, football is my opportunity at a full college scholarship."

Oh my. That's personal.

He doesn't give me a chance to respond. "Dance with me."

"In this field?"

He nods. "Why not? No one's watching us." I slide toward him, stopping when my bottom is on the edge. "But it's fine if you don't want to."

"Who says I don't want to?"

A grin spreads as he reaches for my hands. He helps me from his truck and we take a few steps. He pulls me against him and my nerves ignite as we sway to the slightly staticky echo from the truck's radio.

He holds me close while leading. He's a good dancer. I hadn't expected that.

The next song begins and I could die happy right here because it's one of my all-time favorites. I couldn't have planned this better if I'd chosen the music myself.

He leans away so he can see my face. "I haven't heard this song in a long time. What's the name of it?"

"'Kiss Me.'" I know it like the back of my hand. I've listened to it a million times.

"I thought you'd never ask." He releases my hand and waist and places both palms on my face. He pulls me closer for our first kiss but doesn't start at my lips. He teases me first, trailing his lips along my neck below my ear. My whole body tingles. I breathe deeply, lightheaded as he moves lower on my neck and then around to the other side.

When he finishes torturing me, he moves his mouth across my jaw toward my lips. Even his breathing has deepened.

But it's my turn to torment him.

I tease him, pulling my mouth just out of reach each time he advances. He groans after several attempts and suddenly tugs me so close I can't escape. And I don't want to.

His mouth claims mine, and I allow him. He tastes minty, not a trace of smoke, and I'm surprised.

I smile against his lips when he stops. "You tricked me. You said you wouldn't kiss me until I asked you to."

"'Kiss me.' Those were your words. I was only doing what you told me since I know a princess can throw a fit when she doesn't get her way."

We're still standing in the middle of the field so I walk backward, pulling him with me until we're at his truck, my back pressed against the door. "Now I'm telling you to do it again."

He kisses my forehead and each of my cheeks before finally getting to my mouth. He deepens our kiss and takes my breath away. My head spins as I wrap my arms around his shoulders and squeeze tightly. I yank his body hard against mine, crushing my breasts against his chest. I lift my chin, giving him full access to my neck.

The way he makes me feel is insane, like I would let him do anything he wants to me in this moment. I've never felt anything like this in my life.

"Claire, I need a minute."

He steps away and runs his hands through his hair. He takes a deep breath and then blows it out slowly.

"Are you okay?"

He's standing several feet away with his fingers laced over the top of his head, looking up at the night sky. "Yeah, but you may not be if we don't stop now."

His words spark an excitement in me because I understand his meaning. He wants me. Bad. And I realize I don't want to be okay if it means he's going to stop here.

"Can I see you tomorrow?" I'm not thinking straight. I have no idea how I'll pull it off. I only know I want to spend time with him.

"I have to work all day." He has a job. I have no idea what he does but for some reason, that makes him even sexier. "What about tomorrow night?"

Ugh! My family has dinner plans with the Hendersons but I'm not telling him that. "I have a thing. What about Sunday?"

"Sunday's no good for me."

It's apparent that seeing him this weekend isn't in the cards. "Then we'll stick with Monday at second period."

He laughs. "It's a date."

He doesn't kiss or touch me again but I want him to. I look over at him as he drives me home and strongly consider telling him to pull over. I wouldn't mind him showing me how he'd go about making me not okay.

He parks on the street in front of my house. I want to stay with him in his truck talking the rest of the night but he's told me he has to work the next day. I have to let him leave. "I had a wonderful time tonight."

"Me too."

I wait, and hope, he makes a move to kiss me but he doesn't. Maybe that means he's tied in knots, the same as me. "I guess I'll see you on Monday."

I reach for the door lever but he lifts his index finger, cueing me to wait. He races around the truck and opens my door. I could get used to this.

He still doesn't kiss me. "See you Monday."

I go inside with no more kisses since he doesn't make the move. It's unfortunate. I would have liked many, many more. I lean against the front door and touch my lips, remembering the way it felt when his were there.

This night has been enchanting.

He opened my door, contained a sexual frenzy threatening to burn out of control, and waited until I was safely within my house to drive away. Jesse Boone has turned out to be quite the gentlemen.

Who knew?

CHAPTER FIFTEEN

JESSE BOONE

SOMEWHERE BETWEEN POINT A AND POINT B, SOMETHING HAS GONE ASTRAY. Screwing Claire was the perfect vengeance against Forbes but spending time with her has changed everything. I didn't plan on liking her so much—or at all—but I do. I wasn't supposed to become emotionally involved but I have. I drive away from her tonight realizing my heart doesn't care a thing about my original intentions.

She thinks I pulled away because I was on the verge of ravishing her. That much is true but it isn't why I needed to distance myself. I want her in a different kind of way—one I'm not good enough for and requiring me to give more of myself than I'm willing to share.

She was freely giving herself to me tonight. I never expected that. I'm stoked about it—but spooked as well.

Once I'm home, I lie in bed recalling the taste of her skin and the breathless way she allowed me to kiss her. I wanted her more than air in my lungs and that's a problem. It means I've lost sight of the prize. I no longer desire screwing her as a way to get to Forbes. I want her for myself.

I need to get a grip. To have a girl like Claire means allowing her to be a part of my life, and I'm not willing to go there. I can't risk her knowing my past, or even my present. I can't bear seeing my true self in her eyes.

I'm preoccupied with her and the recollection of our night together when I'm at work on Saturday. Earl sees my distraction and asks what's going on. He always offers to talk but I lie and tell him I'm thinking about football. The truth is that an auburn-haired girl is owning all of my thoughts today.

I'm working beneath a truck and clumsily drop a wrench on my head for the third time. I guess Earl's heard all he wants because he shouts for me to come out. I look at him as though I have no idea what he'll say.

"You're going to put your eye out if you keep dropping that wrench in your face." I sit up and wipe my hands on a rag. "I know something is going on. Has Rita done something else to you?"

He'd be furious if he knew she had me selling dope, but that isn't the reason behind today's distraction. "No, Rita is being Rita."

"Then what's up? I know something's wrong. You can't even tighten a bolt without giving yourself a concussion." Earl has been the only stable thing in my life since I started hanging around his shop when I was a kid. He's watched me grow from a young boy sweeping up around his place into the person I am today.

We've never talked about girls. I don't really know how to introduce the topic.

"It's a girl, isn't it?"

I guess he knows me better than I think. "Yeah, it's a girl—one who's too good for me."

"Who says she's too good for you?"

The world. "Anyone you ask."

He puts his hands on his hips and stands over me. "She's the only one that counts. What does she say about it?"

"She says she wants to try things between us to see where it goes." I leave out the part about her being the girlfriend of the guy I despise.

"Sounds reasonable enough, so what's the problem?"

I can't tell him I fell for the girl I'd planned to screw as retaliation against her boyfriend. "She's cut from a different cloth so it'll never work out. She'll hightail it when she figures out the truth."

"What is the truth?"

"She's beautiful and smart and rich so there's no need wasting my time." Or chancing my heart. "I'm not good enough for her."

"Sounds like you aren't giving her much credit. I suspect she deserves a little more since she's said she wants to try a relationship with you. You're being close-minded, boy. You don't want to get hurt—and there's nothing wrong with that—but you'll never know if things could work out if you don't try."

I know this song and dance. The counselor I saw this summer told me I had a problem with letting people in. She said it was a defense mechanism. Imagine that—I feel the need to defend myself.

"You can't spend your life refusing to take a chance on people. Everyone you meet ain't like Twyla and Rita. There are kind people in the world and it sounds like this girl wants to show you a little. Maybe you should let her. If it doesn't work out, it won't be the worst thing in the world."

Maybe he's right—a little bit. "I'll think about it."

Earl turns away, calling back over his shoulder. "I suggest you think about it after you get off work. I'm not sure your head can take you dropping that wrench on it again."

I slide back under the truck, making no promises since all of my thoughts will be of Claire.

I GO to Rita's after work and find a shitload of cars in the yard. It's Saturday so that means her pals will be partying here tonight. No way I'm hanging around, so I go inside and grab a change of clothes without saying a word.

I take off to Dane's house, hoping to find him home. His mom answers the door and invites me inside. She's a nice lady. He complains about the way she babies him but he has no idea how lucky he is. I'd love to have a mom who did that rather than the one who put me to work selling dope.

I go upstairs and knock on Dane's bedroom door. He laughs when he sees me in my work clothes. "Dude, what's with the grease-monkey getup?"

He knows where I work but he's never seen me dressed the part. "I had to work today. Mind if I bum a shower?"

"No problem." I walk into his room and he sits on his bed. I remain standing because I don't want to soil anything with my greasy work clothes. "Got a hot date with Gretchen tonight?"

"No way." I look at him like he's lost his mind. "I'm done with that chick."

"You mean you done her?" He laughs.

I put my hands up. "No way. I'm not touching that with a ten-foot pole."

He looks unconvinced. "What happened to you last night? One minute you were there and the next, you were gone."

I'm not excited about admitting that I agreed to be with Claire behind Forbes's back so I debate telling him the truth. But Dane's cool—and my only friend. "I was with Claire."

His mouth's agape. "No way, dude."

"I was leaving and she asked me to drive her home. We ended up talking until two this morning."

He shakes his head. "You could've been banging Gretchen but instead you chose to talk to Claire half the night? You must really want to get at Forbes bad if you gave up getting laid."

"It wasn't like that. I ditched Gretchen before I knew Claire wanted a ride."

"You lucky bastard. I guess that means you successfully broke up Claire and Forbes?"

I wish. "Not exactly. She asked me to give her time to explore this thing between us before she ends it with him. I agreed, but I don't know if I can stand seeing them together after everything that happened last night."

"What happened?" he asks.

No way he's getting the details. "Things got pretty intense. That's all I'm going to say about it."

He sits, looking amazed. "You and Claire might actually end up together."

I realize the unlikelihood of anything panning out when I see his surprise. "It's never going to happen. She won't break up with him for me."

"Claire wouldn't have left the bonfire with you or allowed things to get 'intense' if it wasn't a possibility. She's not that kind of girl. I think you give yourself far too little credit."

Dane is encouraging me to hope for something that will never happen, but I know better. It's a lesson I learned well early in life—never allow myself to hope for things out of my reach. It's life's cruel joke of lifting you higher before dropping you flat on your ass.

"I guess we'll see."

"I guess so, but you need to get a shower, dude. If Claire smelled you right now, she'd run the other way. You stink."

Working around motor oil is a job hazard. "Thanks a lot. I didn't know that."

"If you smell better when you come out of the shower, you can hang with me and Harrison tonight."

Good. That means I have something to do instead of going home to Rita's. "Cool."

CHAPTER SIXTEEN

CLAIRE DEVERAUX

Payton calls first thing Saturday morning and I half lie. I don't tell her I stayed out with Jesse until two in the morning or about the connection we made. I give her enough information to convince her I've made headway so she won't be suspicious when he seems friendlier with me.

I spend Saturday night with my parents and the Hendersons, but I avoid being alone with Forbes. He knows something isn't right but I find myself not caring because I'm preoccupied with Jesse.

Sunday comes and I still have Jesse and his beautiful baby blues on my mind. I think about the plans he has for the day and worry they might include a girl. I feel a spark of jealousy. I wish I knew where he lived—I would totally drive by to see what's going on.

I'm glad when Monday finally arrives so I can see him again. I beat him to class and notice that the desks are arranged differently. They're in groups of two facing one another. I like it because I can look at him as much as I like.

I take an empty one and dare anyone but Jesse to try to sit across from me. He takes his sweet time getting to class but when he enters, he sees me and smiles before sitting to face me. My heart skips a beat.

"Hey, you."

He puts his backpack on the floor. "Hey, princess." We're both grinning. "Did you have a good weekend?"

"I had a fabulous Friday." The rest of my weekend wasn't so great. "And yours?

He smiles and it's beautiful. "It had a strong start but went downhill after that. However, I'm optimistic this week will be better."

I lift an eyebrow in curiosity. "You should ask the magic eight ball. It always has an answer."

When he leans closer, his masculine fragrance invades my nose. "I thought I'd ask you instead."

I understand his meaning but I want to hear him say the words. "Ask me what?"

He lowers his voice. "If you would spend time with me. We have exploring to do."

I agree. We have a lot to discover about this secret relationship and I'm looking forward to it. "I'd like that very much."

Mrs. Tanner shuts the classroom door and tells us we'll be finishing up with our last creative ingredient today. She gives us our assignment card and I push it in Jesse's direction. "You read it today."

He opens the envelope and reads aloud, "'Making or seeing connections is bringing together seemingly unrelated ideas, objects, or events in a way that leads to new understanding. Making connections is at the heart of learning. Figuring out what's the same, what's different, and what kind of unusual connections are at the core of creativity. To better acquaint yourself with your partner, compile a list of similarities and differences so you may compare them.'" Jesse places the assignment on my desk. "There's a suggestion list if you'd like to read it over."

I take the list and allow my fingers to graze his. I look into his eyes and what I see there makes me want to touch him more. So I do.

Our hands are concealed from our classmates behind my backpack so I lace my fingers through his; he squeezes them in response. It only lasts a brief moment but the feel of his skin on mine is worth the chance of being seen.

I sigh at the loss of contact when our hands part and look at the list of suggestions. I read the one at the top of the list. "'Compare your family dynamics.'"

CHAPTER SEVENTEEN

JESSE BOONE

FAMILY DYNAMICS AREN'T SOMETHING I'LL SHARE WITH CLAIRE. THE REAL Jesse Boone isn't a person she'd want to know. Hearing about his life would be awkward and uncomfortable, so I decide to tell her things that are easy to hear—even if I'm not telling the whole truth.

As I have no intention of going first, I ask her to tell me about her perfect world. I need time to create my fictitious life portraying a seemingly comfortable lot—one that doesn't draw sympathy or humiliate me.

"I live with both of my parents and I am the youngest of three children. My dad is a physician, an OB-GYN, and my mom is a clinical psychologist. I have one brother, Ryan. He's the oldest. He's in medical school at UT and I have an older sister, Maggie. She's a CRNA."

Nope. No way I'm telling her I live with my dope-dealing grandmother because my mom was shot and killed in a drug deal gone wrong or that her killers shot me and left me for dead while my two little brothers hid in a closet. "I live with both of my parents and I was the only one in the litter. My dad is a mechanic. He runs a garage and body shop so I know a lot about fixing vehicles. My mom is a hairdresser."

She reaches up to touch the front of my hair. "So that's why you have great hair?"

"You think I have great hair?" I play along with the lie I've just told.

She doodles on loose-leaf paper and smiles. "Maybe." She seems embarrassed. "Moving on ... 'Compare your after-graduation plans.'"

There's only one logical guess since everyone in her family works in the medical field. "Let me guess—doctor or nurse?"

She laughs. "Hell no. That would be the biggest fail of all time. I'd kill somebody my first day on the job." She stops laughing and a serious expression replaces her smile as she leans forward and lowers her voice. "I'm going to be a pole dancer."

An image of Claire spinning on a pole in nothing but a G-string and pumps forms. It's a vision I can't unsee—nor do I want to. "Are you saying that to make me fantasize about you on a pole? If so, then mission accomplished." This is not the place for me to tent my pants.

"If it doesn't work out professionally, then I plan to have a pole in my house."

I swallow hard and squeak, "Will you marry me?"

She laughs, dismissing my marriage proposal. "If the pole thing doesn't work out, I'm going to fall back on social work."

Whoa. That's unexpected.

I'd had my fair share of dealings with social workers and knew for a fact that they worked very hard and made little money for the crap they deal with. "Why social work?" Or any profession that had the word "worker" in it since that's a clear indicator you'll work hard for basically no money.

"Adoption holds a special place in my heart since my brother, sister, and I are adopted. I want to help kids in need find good homes." This girl just keeps surprising me. "My parents adopted Ryan from Russia and Maggie from China. They thought their family was complete with a boy and girl but then I came along unexpectedly. The woman who gave birth to me came into the hospital where my father worked, pushed out a heroin-addicted baby, and left. No one wanted me because I was so sick from all the things she did during the pregnancy. My parents were the only ones willing to take me in."

She and I are cut from the same cloth after all, but her outcome is so much better than mine. Do Forbes and the others know her backstory? "Don't look so sad, Jesse. This princess's fairytale has a happy ending. I'm okay."

She's mistaken. I'm not at all sad for her. I'm angry with myself. She shared a special part of herself with me—something real—and I gave her nothing but a big, fat lie.

She pokes me in the arm. "Please cheer up because the look on your face is really bringing me down."

I force a smile. "Sorry. I don't mean to be a drag. I'm just surprised is all."

She smiles and changes the subject—probably to ease the discomfort. "So, what do you want to be when you grow up?"

I feel the need to lighten the mood. "I'm going to be a tattoo artist. Much like pole dancing, it's an underappreciated art form. I became interested a few months ago when I got my first one." I'm sure she's seen my tat but I pull my sleeve up so she can get a better view. "What do you think?"

She reaches out to trace my ink. "I love it."

Her combined words and touch set me on fire. I don't think she could have turned me on more if she'd flipped my on switch. But class isn't where this needs to happen so I try to play it cool and move on to a less stimulating topic. "When I'm not sticking needles with ink into people, I'm going to be an attorney—but not the sleazy kind. I want to prosecute the guilty, not defend them." Yeah. It's ironic considering the laws I break selling drugs.

She frowns. "That's a bummer. You'll have to wear a suit and it'll cover that little beauty."

"I might be mistaken for the criminal if I don't cover them."

She studies the design. "Them? Does that mean you're going to get another one?"

I point to the area I plan on doing next. "Yeah, I'm going to take this part down closer to my elbow."

"Can I go with you when you do it?" Again, this girl surprises me.

I'm not sure how I'd feel having her by my side while I'm getting inked, but I'd like to find out. "You can if you want. Do I need to make an appointment for two?" I wish I could take her this week. I'd love to see her reaction.

"Umm ... no. I would only be observing."

The rest of humanities flies. History does as well but then physics comes and I'm forced to endure Claire sitting with Forbes. I hate it. I want her all to myself but at least they sit behind me so I don't have to look at them the whole hour.

Classes finally over, I go to the field for practice. Our first game is Friday. That means Forbes has four days to take me out. I wonder if today's the day.

I dress out and remind myself to be on guard. I must be mindful at all times to prevent myself from getting hurt. After two hours of practice, we're all worn out and I allow myself to relax when I decide he can't possibly have the energy to try blitzing me.

I turn to see Claire before the next play and watch her get tossed into the air much higher than I like. My heart pauses until I see her feet safely on the ground. I breathe a sigh of relief and that's when it happens.

All I see is many shades of black.

CHAPTER EIGHTEEN

CLAIRE DEVERAUX

THIRTY MINUTES OF PRACTICE REMAINS BEFORE I'M FREE TO SNEAK AWAY FOR A little exploratory time with Jesse—that is, if I find a way to get rid of Forbes. I think of the different scenarios and decide I might have to resort to the aid of my bestie, even if it means lying to her.

My cheer partners gather around for another basket toss but Payton is preoccupied with something going on out on the field. "What are you looking at?"

"Looks like somebody got smoked. Maybe it's Forbes," Payton says. I look to see what she's talking about. The entire team is crowded in a circle, looking down. Both coaches are on the ground and that's when we realize a player is injured.

Harrison runs toward the field house but doesn't answer when Payton asks what's happening. That must mean it's bad.

Dane looks at me and then back toward the player on the ground. He does it a second time and then motions for me to come over. "It's Jesse. Forbes took a cheap shot at him and now he's down and isn't getting up. He's out cold and they can't wake him." My heart accelerates. "It's been a few minutes and he hasn't responded, so the coaches sent Harrison to call for an ambulance."

99

I push through the crowd and see him lying motionless on the ground, Coach Osborne by his side. Coach calls Jesse's name repeatedly and gives him verbal commands, but it's in vain.

Harrison returns with a cell phone and holds it out. "Coach, they want to talk to you."

Coach Osborne looks at me. "Claire, hold his hand and talk to him while I tell the dispatcher what happened."

I drop to my knees at his side. "Jesse, it's Claire. Can you open your eyes for me?" Panic sets in when he doesn't reply. "Jesse, try to open your eyes."

I squeeze his hand and pray he'll wake up soon. Every passing minute is crucial so I lean down to whisper in his ear. "Hey, you. It's princess and I really need you to look at me."

I sit back on my feet to watch his face. His eyelids flutter, so I lean down again. "Open those beautiful blue eyes for me."

I lift my face and this time see his piercing blues looking up at me. "Hey, you. Glad to see you're back. You checked out on us for a few minutes."

"What happened?" he asks.

"I'm not sure. I saw a crowd standing around you and Dane called me to come over because you were out cold."

Jesse's teammates see that he's come around and they begin dispersing.

"You scared me," I whisper.

"It was a little scary to wake up to a hovering crowd."

"It took a couple of minutes of holding your hand and talking to you before you came around."

He looks happy. "You talked to me and held my hand in front of everyone—even Forbes?"

"Yeah." I think he may still be a bit confused. "I did and I'm still holding your hand in front of everyone, silly."

"You sure?" He lifts his head to look down. "I can't feel you holding my hand."

What? I give it a firm squeeze to prove it. "See?"

A frightened look comes over his face and his breathing

increases. "I didn't feel that at all."

I use my fingernails to pinch his skin, hard enough to leave an indentation. "What about that?"

"Nothing." He looks up at the sky. "I can't feel any of that."

I see his fear and realization forms in my head. "There's an ambulance on the way. Don't try to move at all, especially your head and neck."

He's trying to be brave. I see it on his face. "What about your leg?" I reach down and pinch his right thigh as hard as I can, terrified he'll tell me he can't feel it.

"Shit!" he shouts and I've never been happier to hear someone cuss. "That's going to leave a mark."

"Sorry." I touch his arm and leg on the left side of his body. "Everything on this side feels normal?"

"I think so." That's reassuring.

I feign a confident face while pure terror brews on the inside. "Don't worry. It's going to be fine."

An ambulance arrives and a cervical collar is immediately placed on Jesse's neck, making this a little too surreal. He's loaded into the back and taken away.

I avoid Forbes, disappearing through the crowd to get to my car. There's no way I'm not going to the hospital.

I'm surprised when I'm allowed into the ER to see him. Where are his parents? They should be contacted.

I stand back until the rush to assess him is over. Once we're alone, I take his hand—the one with feeling—in mine. "Your parents need to be called. I'm happy to do it if you'll give me their number."

"They're out of town."

"They'll want to know what's happened." I reach into my purse and take out a pad and pen. "You need someone to be here with you. Give me a number so I can notify a family member or friend."

The way he looks at me is strange. I don't know what it means. "Jesse? Are you all right?"

He doesn't have an opportunity to answer because two men

come into the room and wheel him away for tests. I'm left alone, with an blank notepad, unsure what to do. I'm certain Coach Osborne and the team will be in the waiting room wanting an update, but I choose to stay put until I have answers.

It's an eternity, I'm sure of it, while I sit waiting and praying. I imagine every possible scenario but they all end with the same thought. I curse myself for not being more optimistic but it's hard.

Jesse finally returns from testing and the staff pushes his bed against the wall. "Good news. I started feeling my arm while they were running tests. I can move it now. See?"

He reaches for my hand and takes it in his. I bring it to my face and stroke it along my cheek. "You can feel me?"

"Yeah. My whole arm burns like hellfire but it's better than feeling nothing." He sounds optimistic.

I squeeze it tightly. "And this?"

"Yes."

I move higher to his tattoo and drag my nails downward. "And that?"

"Yep."

Relief floods me and I lean forward to place my forehead against his. I close my eyes and thank God for allowing him to be okay. "I was so scared."

He reaches up and places his hand on the back of my neck, holding me securely so I can't back away—not that I want to. "I was too. Terrified, actually. I thought my arm was paralyzed for sure."

His warm breath tickles my lips for a moment and I give in to the urge to kiss him. We don't feel close enough so I leave my chair and sit on the edge of his hospital bed. His hands travel down my back and he pulls me nearer.

I could do this with him forever and never be satiated.

Someone clears his voice from the doorway. I'm both annoyed and embarrassed to be interrupted.

It's my father standing there, bewildered. Holy shit.

"Umm ... I was in between cases and heard you were down here with a friend, so I thought I would check in. Is everything all right?"

I'm so busted.

I pull my hand from Jesse's as I stand. "Dad, this is Jesse Boone. We go to school together. He took a hit on the field today and was unconscious for a while. He couldn't feel his arm when he came to, but the sensation is back now."

"Sounds like a stinger if you've spontaneously regained the feeling and use of it. Those are somewhat common in football players. It should be fine with no permanent damage if that's all it is. I know Coach Osborne will be relieved to know his starting quarterback isn't out for the season." He knows about Jesse?

"Yes, sir. I consider myself very lucky."

My father's eyes float to Jesse's tattoo peeking out from his hospital gown. I wince internally. This is definitely not the way I would've wanted my dad to meet Jesse.

Dad's pager buzzes. "I've got a patient on the table so I need to run. It was nice to meet you, Jesse." Dad gives me a look that says we'll discuss this later. Double holy shit. "I'll see you at home this evening, Claire."

"Nice to meet you, Dr. Deveraux."

My dad gone, I realize I've been holding my breath. Jesse exhales loudly. "That was awkward." Jesse doesn't strike me as the type who'd be comfortable doing the parent thing.

"I'm sorry. That's not how I would've planned that at all."

"Does that mean you would want me to meet your parents?" he asks.

The thought of Jesse coming to my house to meet my family stirs butterflies in my stomach, making me both nervous and excited. "I would want you to meet them if we started dating. Wouldn't you want me to meet your family if things moved forward between us?"

There it is again—that strange look.

"Right now, I think you should be more concerned with how you're going to explain to your father why you were making out with me. I highly doubt he's going to believe it was CPR."

"I was not making out with you." Yeah, I totally was.

"I'm sure it looked that way from where he stood. You were

practically assaulting me."

Oh God. He's right. I have some explaining to do. But … will I choose safe and comfortable by staying with Forbes so I don't rock the boat, or go with Jesse and face a potentially explosive outcome?

CHAPTER NINETEEN

JESSE BOONE

I SHOULD BE PLOTTING ALL THE WAYS I'LL USE CLAIRE AGAINST FORBES—especially since he tried to paralyze me—but I'm not. I care nothing about vengeance when I look at the princess. My affection for her overrules any bad intentions I have against Henderson. But I won't substitute tolerance for ignorance. The bastard could've killed me with a hit like that.

I admit I no longer want Claire as retribution against her boyfriend. I've fallen in love with her and now I have to figure out how to convince her she belongs with me.

The exam curtain slides aside and the ER doctor enters. "Mr. Boone, the nurses tell me you've regained feeling in your arm. That's good news and supports the diagnosis of a nerve injury called a stinger. We typically see it in football players." He comes over and unfastens the tie on my hospital gown, lowering it to my chest. "I'm just going to take a quick look."

I'm halfway shirtless in front of Claire and she has no shame in checking me out, which means she'll see my scar. "Hey, Doc, can you explain what a stinger is?"

"It can happen one of two ways. Either your head and neck are forced downward against your shoulder and the nerves leading from the spinal cord to that arm are compressed." He demonstrates by moving his own head and neck. "The other possibility is that your head and neck were forced away from the shoulder, causing those nerves to be stretched. But no worries. Yours is minor and I expect a full recovery since it's your right arm. An injury to the left could've been devastating so soon after the previous trauma."

Shit. She's going to ask about it.

No time to worry about that. "I can't miss Friday's game."

He laughs at my eagerness. "You should probably take tomorrow off. I think it'll be fine to resume practice on Wednesday but I want to observe you a couple more hours. I think we can get you home if everything still looks all right at that time."

"Thank you."

I'm lucky. If Forbes knew the damage he could've caused my other shoulder, he would've sacked me from the other side.

"What kind of trauma have you had?"

I knew that was coming.

It doesn't matter that the doctor mentioned my injury. There's no way Claire didn't see my scar when the EMTs cut my jersey off.

There's no way I'm telling her it's from a gunshot wound. She'll want to know the circumstances leading up to it. "I tore the rotator cuff in my shoulder. I've had some surgeries to repair it."

"That sounds painful."

"Let's just say I don't recommend it."

She sits on my bed again, stroking her fingertips down my arm. "Two hours. What are we going to do while we wait?"

"Hmm ... any ideas?"

"I can think of one thing." Her mouth connects with mine and we pick up where we left off before her dad came around.

CLAIRE'S SITTING next to me in the bed. "Would you like me to take you home when you're released?"

There's was no way that's happening. Claire will never come

within ten miles of the trailer park where I live if I have anything to do with it. "I got so caught up in you, I forgot to call Earl. I should probably do that since he's the one keeping an eye on me while my parents are out of town."

"Who's Earl?" she asks.

"My boss."

"At your dad's garage?" Oh hell. I forgot about that lie.

I need to get my shit straight or I'll be busted for sure. "Yeah. He's probably going to be pissed I haven't called and I don't want to make things worse by not letting him give me a ride."

"Okay. I don't want you to be in trouble."

The nurse comes in to remove my IV. I call Earl as soon as she finishes. He's pretty hacked off because I didn't let him know sooner, but he'll get over it.

My nurse comes back to give discharge instructions and Claire steps to the waiting room to update Coach Osborne and the team.

I'm finishing up with release papers when Earl comes into my room. "Jesse, you should've called me when this happened."

Now I feel bad I didn't. "Everything happened really fast and I wasn't thinking clearly when I got here. I took a hard lick but they say I'm going to be fine." I lift my arm and flex my hand to prove I have full use of it. "I've already gotten the feeling back."

"Someone should've been with you."

"I wasn't alone. Claire was with me."

Claire walks through the door just in time to hear Earl ask, "Is Claire the girl you couldn't stop thinking about when you almost broke your face with a wrench?"

I wince because I know I'll be explaining that one later. "Yes, sir, the very same girl who's standing behind you right now."

There's only time for a brief introduction before my nurse returns with a wheelchair. "Do I have to ride in that? It was my arm that was hurt. I'm able to walk fine."

She gives me an understanding smile. "How 'bout I have the ambassador walk you out?" That's more like it.

Earl goes out to get his pickup while a woman leads me and

Claire to the discharge exit. "I sent everyone away so you wouldn't have to deal with them. I hope that's all right." It's more than fine.

I reach for her hand. "I could kiss you."

"And I'd like you to but we're in the middle of the emergency room waiting area, so I doubt it's appropriate."

The ambassador wishes me her best as she leaves us at the exit waiting for Earl to pull around.

"Is there anything I can do for you—drive your truck home or pick you up for school in the morning?"

Hell no!

It's a shame I can't allow myself to become close to this girl because she sure is making it easy. "Earl's gonna drop me at the field to get my truck. But thanks for the offer."

We say our goodbyes when my chauffeur pulls up and I take comfort in knowing I'll see my princess again in less than eleven hours.

THOUGHTS OF CLAIRE rob me of sleep. There is no mistaking the incredible chemistry between us, but this isn't about sexual attraction. I know what that feels like, and this is so much more. It's something I've never experienced in my life.

At the hospital, she held my hand while we waited to learn my fate, good or bad. She stayed—that's something I can't say about anyone in my life—so it means something to me.

I go to the kitchen for breakfast and Rita isn't sitting at the table. I'm glad since my injury and visit to the hospital prevented me from peddling her dope. I don't want an ass-chewing first thing this morning. I get ready as fast as I can without making too much noise and shoot out the door before she wakes and busts my chops about her money.

My escape from Rita lands me at school early, so I park. I flick my lighter and recall the day Claire told me I didn't care about my health and I was too weak to quit smoking.

I put the cigarette away as I consider all the reasons to quit. I know I'll never find a better one than her.

I pop a piece of gum into my mouth and crack my calculus book while waiting for the hands of the clock to turn. Students eventually begin arriving. Payton pulls into the parking spot behind me. I'm briefly excited until I remember Claire won't be with her.

I turn my attention back to math and hear a knock on the window of my passenger door. It's Payton so I lean over to raise the lock. She swings the door open and gets in without waiting for an invitation.

"Please, join me." I motion with my hand for her to have a seat, although she's already inside.

"I'm glad I ran into you. We need to talk about Claire—in private."

"Umm … I don't think it's going to get much more private than this."

"Are you falling for Claire?" Damn. This girl is bold.

I don't know how much Payton knows about my agreement with Claire, so I don't know which way to go with my answers. They're best friends but I don't want to assume too much. "Why do you want to know?"

"I'm her best friend so I'm aware that you've agreed to try things out, but I need to know if I should encourage this relationship or not. If you're using her to get at Forbes, then it stops here. If you're truly falling for her, that's a different story entirely. She's into you, but I won't sit back and watch her get hurt." I get it. Another warning.

I hesitate because admitting feelings and emotions isn't my thing.

She searches my face. "You are, aren't you?"

I shrug and play dumb. "What?"

She sounds astonished. "You don't have to tell me because I see it. You're falling for my girl. This isn't a game to you."

I don't deny her claim, therefore proving her allegation. I am falling for Claire. I'm growing more and more vulnerable to her— something I've never allowed myself to do.

Payton is the only person, besides Claire, who can answer the question on my mind. I decide to stop hiding behind the wall I've built around myself. "Am I crazy for thinking I could have a chance with her?"

CHAPTER TWENTY

CLAIRE DEVERAUX

I DON'T MAKE IT COMPLETELY OUT OF MY HOMEROOM DOORWAY BEFORE Payton yanks me to the corner. "You little sly slut puppy. I am extraordinarily proud of you."

"Am I missing something?"

"I knew you could get Jesse Boone to lust after you. I even dared to hope you'd convince him to date you, but I never dreamed you'd manage to make him fall for you. Congratulations." What is she talking about? "The power you hold over him is crazy good. You exceeded my expectations. This is such a tattooable moment. Pun completely intended."

Is she rattling off about me going to the hospital with him? "He has not fallen for me. Why would you think that?"

"I talked to him this morning and got the official status," she squeals.

I give her a shove—maybe a little too hard—and she stumbles backward. "Shut the front door. Where, when, how, why? I need details."

"Where? Parking lot. When? This morning before school. How? In his truck. Why? Because I wanted to see the progress you've made."

My heart is racing. "Omigod."

"I straight up asked if he was falling for you. He didn't give me an answer but a blind man could clearly see that he has. I told him I saw it on his face and he didn't deny it. He asked me if he had a chance with you."

I'm thrilled to know this but I wish Payton didn't. It's only going to set her on fire to push forward with the plan to annihilate Jesse. "What did you say?"

"I told him to go for it because you like-like him. Claire, this couldn't be going more perfectly if I'd orchestrated it myself."

"You did orchestrate it yourself." And I wish she hadn't. This is going to blow up in my face.

She cackles. "I know."

Payton and I are both thrilled with Jesse's feelings toward me but for completely different reasons. Hearing that he's falling for me as well changes everything.

I'm anxious about seeing Jesse but disappointed when I remember we finished our creative ingredients assignment. I'll miss that one-on-one time with him. I really hope Mrs. Tanner will begin another partnering project.

I enter humanities and find the desks have been returned to a circle instead of groups of two. I take a seat and Jesse sits next to me only a minute later. "Hey, princess."

"Hey, you. The arm's still good?" I reach out to touch it—partly because I need him to tell me he feels my touch but also because I can't resist feeling my skin against his.

He brings his free hand up and cups it over mine grasping his bicep. "Good as new." He flexes his muscle a few times to prove it.

Swoon.

"I thought about you all night." Wow. That sounds desperate. I can't believe I said that. "I mean … I was worried about your arm."

"I thought about you all night too … but it wasn't your arm on my mind."

Double swoon.

His words send me into orbit. "What kind of thoughts were you having about me?"

"I'll be keeping that to myself."

Mrs. Tanner begins class and announces that we'll spend the next few days in the library doing research on the lyrics behind Billy Joel's song, "We Didn't Start the Fire." I couldn't be happier since partnering is encouraged.

In the library, we choose a computer in the back, distancing ourselves from our classmates. "This is surprisingly secluded. I could take advantage of you and no one would know."

I lift an eyebrow. "Promise?"

He places his hand on my leg and leans over so his mouth is against my ear. "I'm talking about stealing your answers, dirty girl."

I love this game of naughty insinuation. "We have an assignment. We should probably get on it."

That mischievous grin belonging only to him appears. I love it. "Yes. We should definitely get it on. I mean … get on it. The assignment, that is."

I playfully slap his leg. "You're the dirty one here, not me."

Once we're started on the assignment, I catch Jesse staring at me. Suddenly self-conscious, I run my palms down each of my cheeks. "What are you looking at? Do I have something on my face?"

"You do." He reaches out, grazing the back of his fingers against my cheek. "You've got a little beautiful right there."

The heat rises because I'm not used to such direct compliments. Forbes doesn't do romantic. He's too busy planning how he'll get what he wants from me.

"You want to kiss me, don't you?" God, do I ever.

He's daring—and I love it—so I decide to return the boldness. "You have no idea how much."

He isn't going to back down. I see his determination but as I recall, he warned me about that. "I bet I have a pretty good idea since I probably want to kiss you just as much. Maybe more."

We're alone—most likely safe from being seen—but not

guaranteed so it makes it so much more exciting. The thrill of being caught by someone makes my heart pump faster. I look into his pale blue eyes, willing him to lean forward and take the kiss I'm prepared to give him.

"I'll do it," he threatens.

"Then stop talking about it." I know the sure-fire way to seal the deal. "I dare you."

Bingo. I see it in his eyes. He's in full-on badass mode. "I warned you I don't back down."

"That's what I'm counting on."

I imagine him leaning forward to steal a quick kiss but he doesn't. He takes my hand and leads me across the library. He looks in every direction before opening a door and pulling me into a storage room I didn't know existed. He shuts the door behind us and locks it.

Oh God. What's he going to do?

He places his hands around my waist and pulls me close, our faces almost touching. "Believe me yet?"

"No. I need more proof."

"I was hoping you'd say that."

He places sweet, soft kisses on my lips and my legs threaten to crumble beneath me. His mouth migrates to my neck and up to my ear where he sucks my lobe. I let him because I know the door is locked.

My breath is ragged as his kisses become more urgent ... until someone jiggles the door knob from the other side. I giggle and he cups his hand over my mouth while shushing me. "Quiet. Do you want to get caught?"

I'm feeling a rebellious streak so I don't care if we do. I'm having too much fun.

Whoever it is goes away. "Come on, princess. We better get out before whoever that is comes back with a key."

He cracks the door and peeks out, making sure the coast is clear. Once he's certain we won't be seen, he opens the door and we sprint toward our table. I giggle all the way back because I'm high from the excitement of almost being caught.

Mrs. Tanner rounds on us only moments after we're back at our table to check our progress. "You two are quite a bit behind the others. You need to pick up the pace."

"Yes, ma'am," we say in unison and laugh after she walks away. We're definitely picking up the pace, just not the way she intends.

"Okay, we're going to get a low grade if we don't get serious," he says. "Don't make me regret allowing you to be my partner."

"You think you allowed me to be your partner? I can arrange for Brad to swap with me. In fact, I bet I could find him right now and talk him into it."

I stand, pretending I'll walk away. He reaches for my arm and tugs, pulling me onto his lap. "I have no doubt you could talk Brad into doing anything for you."

This is crazy. I can't be sitting on his lap at school, yet I don't get up immediately. I look around and give him a quick kiss before returning to my chair.

We get a little more serious about our work since we're behind and I realize something. Jesse is smart … like, really smart. We don't have to look up a lot of the things listed in the lyrics because he already knows what they mean. "How do you know all this stuff? You're like a walking, breathing search engine."

"How do you not know this stuff? It's history. Every one of these things listed in the lyrics made headlines."

"Peyton Place. I've heard that term used but I've never known what it means."

"It's a novel from the fifties about people in a small town hiding their sordid secrets—incest, abortion, adultery, lust, murder. You name it, it's in Peyton Place. They even made it into a movie and television series. Highly controversial."

Jesse continues to both enlighten and amaze me with his knowledge of world events. It isn't his intention but he makes me look like less than the top student in school.

In third period, we sit in the same seats we've taken since the first day of school. "Am I doing better?"

He turns his head and whispers over his shoulder, "Better at what?"

I lean forward, hoping he feels my breath on his neck. "You told me I should smile more. I've been working on it."

"Yes. It suits you." It's true. The smiles are because of him.

"I'm not looking forward to next period." I hear the pain in his voice and I'm no longer smiling.

Nothing has changed between me and Forbes. I thought he'd be furious with me for holding Jesse's hand and talking him through his injury but he didn't mention it, so I didn't either. It seems he was so full of himself following the assault, he didn't notice me with Jesse.

There's no decision to be made between the two. I know who I want but I'm chickenshit about ending things with Forbes because I'm still that girl—the one petrified of what everyone will say.

Physics is brutal for more than one reason. Forbes is by my side and Jesse isn't. He's next to Gretchen and I suspect she's purposely flicking my come-apart switch by constantly touching him. If it's not his arm, it's his leg or his back and shoulders.

Is she aware how much she's getting to me?

I slip further into her trap every time she touches him but I lose it when she starts talking sexy time. "Those jeans look really good on you but they'd look even better on my bedroom floor."

I have a slip in my impulse control and can't take hearing her mouth anymore. "Gretchen, Jesse doesn't want to swap bodily fluids with you so stop harassing him."

Forbes huffs. "Not this again, Claire. Their screw-a-thon is not your business."

I think Gretchen has figured out my feelings for Jesse and this is her way of taunting me. It's only a matter of time before she busts me.

This can't go on for much longer. It's driving me crazy. I have to do something. Soon—by this weekend.

CHAPTER TWENTY-ONE

JESSE BOONE

I'M WALKING TO THE FIELD AND A THOUGHT CROSSES MY MIND. I NEED TO thank Gretchen for that little stunt she pulled in physics, even if it was for her own pleasure. I have to give props where they're deserved. The penivore definitely has a gift for getting under Claire's skin. I enjoyed Claire's little display of possessiveness and although I've given up my raid on Forbes, I hope he enjoyed seeing his girlfriend come to my defense.

I'm not looking forward to sitting on the bench in practice today but I'm following doctor's orders—the temporary loss of feeling in my arm scared me shitless. It was a terror I've known only one other time in my life.

Yesterday's incident brought back old memories and fears—things I'd like to tell Claire but I can't. I'm not there yet but I'm making progress. I've shared small parts of myself with the princess and found that I like being vulnerable to her.

She's gotten more out of me than anyone—except my psych counselor, Dr. Deandra Wesson. She knows everything.

It's been a month since I saw Deandra, and I miss our sessions—or maybe it's the human connection I miss. I'm not sure but I feel like I'm building a bond with Claire that would rival any connection I had with Deandra. My princess has the power to heal me.

Damn. I don't know how those thoughts snuck into my head.

I turn my attention to my pretty, auburn-haired girl. She's getting ready to be tossed into the air and I brace myself as she flies upward and then back down again into a cradle of arms. I breathe a sigh of relief, as I always do, when her feet are planted safely on the ground.

"Dude, you're being blatantly obvious with your staring," Dane warns. "You have drool down the front of your shirt."

He's right, minus the drooling. I'm not hiding my interest in Claire well because it's too easy to pretend there is no Forbes Henderson. "I can't help it."

Since Dane's here, I'm going to take this opportunity to apologize. "I'm sorry I didn't listen to you about Henderson. I really didn't think he was a threat but you were right. That son of a bitch could've killed me."

Dane stretches his leg. "I know him and I'm shocked at how far he took it. But he'll have to lay off for now. Everyone knows he's the one who hit you, so he'll be watched."

"Yeah. Lightning never strikes twice in the same place."

"Right. Are you going to say anything to him?"

"No point since I can't lay a hand on him." The authorities have kept an eye on me since the shooting. I was a minor then but they don't believe I was an innocent bystander. I'm sure they're anxious for the day they can charge me with something, but it won't be assault on Forbes Henderson. I'm too smart for that. "I'm going to let him squirm with the anticipation of how I will execute my payback."

"That's your best bet." Dane takes a quick drink of water. "My parents are out of town on their annual anniversary trip so I'm having a party at my house after the game Friday night. Think you can make it?"

"Sounds like fun."

"Claire's invited. Are you going to ask her to come with you?"

That's a sticky situation. "I don't know. She hasn't broken up with Forbes and although I promised her time to decide, I'm ready to tell her to choose. Seeing them together is making me crazy." I can't believe I'm sitting around waiting for her to decide if she wants me or that jackass. There's no way I would do this for anyone else.

"She's afraid to abandon the comfort zone. Don't worry, it'll work out. I've seen the way she looks at you. It's only a matter of time."

I appreciate his support but I'm not feeling so assured. "I wish I had your confidence."

"Uh-oh," he says. "Coach just spotted me. Gotta jet."

I watch the current play with Forbes acting as quarterback. Even I have to admit that he isn't terrible but he doesn't have it where it counts. His heart isn't in the game.

The cheerleaders finish practice and I watch Claire as she leaves the field. "You just can't keep your eyes off my girlfriend, can you, skank?"

I swivel toward the sound of his voice. I want to punch him in his smug face and break his nose but I can't lay a finger on him. Doesn't stop me from taunting him.

"What are you going to do about it? Take another cheap shot?"

"That's what I did last time I caught you watching my girl," he laughs. He's so very proud of what he did to me. "Maybe next time you won't be so lucky."

He's nothing more than a coward. Guys like him remind me of Wayne, and that makes me fearful of what he might do to Claire, especially if he finds out what we're doing behind his back. I don't want her around him anymore.

THE NEXT COUPLE of days fly because I'm falling so quickly. Claire and I enjoy this game we've become so fluent at playing but I'm growing tired of the charade. I've decided I'm giving her an ultimatum at Dane's party. I hope she doesn't tell me to screw off.

We're sitting in the library finishing our research and I reach for her hand, something she's grown accustomed to at our private table at the back. "I need to talk to you."

She looks up from her work and places her pencil on the table, giving me her full attention. "Sounds serious."

"It is to me." It's more serious than I ever thought I could be about a girl.

"I'm listening."

I search for the words I've rehearsed a thousand times, but they're scattered. I'm saying what I feel in my heart. "It's been a week." My voice sounds dry and squeaky.

"Yes, it has," she says.

I clear my throat. "I know I told you I would give you the time you needed but I've changed my mind. I can't stand seeing you with him anymore. It's making me crazy, so I'm asking you to decide between us."

"I've made my decision and I was planning to talk it over with you tonight at Dane's." Tonight will be the beginning of something incredible or the end of something memorable.

The thought of never kissing her again makes my chest tight. How will I cope if she doesn't choose me? I need one last shot at convincing her I'm the right choice.

I take her by the hand and pull her into the storage room, locking the door behind us. I hold her face in my hands and kiss her like I never will again. She wraps her arms around my neck and pulls me close, making me wonder if she's taking advantage of this as our last kiss.

She lifts her chin and I move my lips down her neck, willing her to choose me instead of him. Her breathing grows faster and I can't imagine never having her in my arms like this again.

I press my forehead to hers. "Choose me, princess. Not him." I hear the desperation in my voice and I'm unashamed. "I'm tormented by thoughts of not being together because I've fallen so deeply in love with you."

She takes my face in her hands and looks into my eyes—saying nothing—and that's the moment I know. She's picking him.

The bell rings and I'm snapped from my daze.

"The bell rang," she says.

"I don't want to move."

"Meet me at Dane's tonight and we'll talk."

Her words are neither reassuring nor ominous. It's going to be a long twelve hours. "I'll be there, princess."

I flee to the refuge of my truck as soon as my last class ends. I need a cigarette so badly, but I resist the urge. Because of Claire. Because she despises cigarettes. So they will no longer be a part of who I am because my mind is made up. No matter her decision, I won't stop until she's mine.

CHAPTER TWENTY-TWO

CLAIRE DEVERAUX

I WAS SO CLOSE TO CONFESSING TO JESSE IN THE STORAGE ROOM, BUT THAT isn't how or where I want him to find out. We need privacy and a school library doesn't fit the bill.

I recall how miserable he looked and I hate knowing I'm the cause. I've asked too much of him and now I'm making him wait until tonight.

He's in love with me. So very deeply—his words.

Swoon.

I arrive at the game and the players are already on the field warming up. My eyes immediately seek Jesse, the number "7" stretched across the back of his jersey. I'm in another world as I watch him throw to Cooper.

Payton startles me from behind. "I think you should punk him tonight. He's admitted to being in love with you so there's nothing to be gained by taking this any further. It's a waste of your time and energy, and I think Dane's party is the perfect place for it to happen since everyone will be there."

I recall his declaration of love and all I want to do is run to him. "I'll think about it." I can't tear my eyes away from him as I lie to my best friend.

"If you don't punk him tonight, you should tell him how much you love him because it's so terribly clear."

"I plan to," I say without thinking.

Oh shit.

Realization hits and I gasp before slapping my hand over my mouth. I want to eat the words, shove them back inside, but it's too late. The wicked trickster duped me into admitting my love for Jesse Boone.

"Good grief, Claire. Did you really think you could fool me? I'm the player who recognizes the game. How could you forget that?"

I panic, trying to decide if I should pretend I was kidding or come clean and own my crazy, beautiful love for Jesse.

I go with my heart. "I didn't mean to fall for him. It just sort of happened as we spent time together."

"Well ... as far as I'm concerned, he's an improvement from Forbes."

"You and I couldn't have been more wrong about who he is. He's a really great guy." Payton looks like she isn't quite sure what to think of me. "I'm telling him that I love him."

"Are you sure you want to jump head first into that?"

"Positive." I debate telling her what he did at school. "He pulled me into the closet in the school library and kissed me until I was senseless. He asked me to choose him over Forbes because he's fallen in love with me."

"What if he's playing you to get at Forbes?" She's looking out for me.

"He's not. I'd know if he were."

THE TEAM IS about to run on to the field and Forbes walks toward me for his traditional good-luck kiss, but I pretend to not see him. I ask Payton to put me up into a shoulder stand so I can avoid the awkwardness of turning him away. The plan works because he changes course and joins the team behind the run-through sign.

I stand on Payton's shoulders holding one side of the sign and my eyes find Jesse in the crowd. He's looking up at me. I mouth, "Good luck."

He smiles and mouths back, "Thanks."

The game is only a few minutes in when East Franklin scores on a sixty-yard pass that Jesse throws to Cooper in the end zone. He does it a second time in the first quarter and then a third before halftime. He throws a fourth completed pass resulting in another touchdown before the end of the last quarter and Dane makes good on every kick. The game is a complete shutout—thirty-five to zero against Nortonville.

Coach Osborne gathers the team for the post-game talk, so Payton and I take the opportunity to hurry to my house to get ready for Dane's party. No way I'm going stinky in my cheerleading uniform.

I change into a casual black dress and sandals before braiding the front of my hair. I fluff the back of my hair after curling it loosely and freshen my makeup before spraying myself with my favorite body spray.

Payton whistles at me. "I hope you know CPR because you are going to take Jesse's breath away."

I do a spin about for Payton. "Do you really think I look okay?"

She nods and lifts her eyebrows. "I think you look awesome and I know Jesse will too. Do you want me to drive so you can leave with him and not have your car stuck at Dane's?"

"That would be so perfect. Sure you don't mind?"

"Not at all." She looks sad but happy at the same time. It's an unusual look for her. "I want you to be happy. If Jesse is the one who does that, then I want you to be with him."

I desperately want Payton's approval so I couldn't be happier. I hug her tightly. "Thank you, Payton. Your support means the world to me."

"Anything for my Claire Bear." She returns my embrace. "Come on. Let's go get your happily ever after on."

We arrive at Dane's and I'm both nervous and excited. Tonight's a game changer.

We go into the foyer and kids are all over the house—some dancing to loud music, others drinking beer from plastic cups. Mrs. Wickham would have a fit if she knew what was going on in her house right now.

I search the crowd for Jesse but don't see him anywhere. My phone alerts me to a new text. It's from Jesse, telling me he's out front waiting for me.

Good. I'm ready for this.

I leave through the front door and I'm nearly running by the time I get to his truck. I'm that excited to see him. "Are you the getaway driver?"

We're parked under the streetlight so I can clearly see the worry on his face. I want to put it to rest but this isn't the place. "I guess I am if you're wanting to get away from here."

I definitely do. ASAP. "Where are you taking me tonight?"

He looks uneasy. "Where do you want to go?"

I smile, hoping to bring him a little reassurance. "I don't have a preference—anywhere but here."

He slowly pulls away from Dane's house. "I have a place in mind but you might think it's a little weird."

My curiosity is piqued. "I can handle that."

"I'm not sure weird is the right word. Maybe unexpected is a better choice."

He cranks the radio to drown the silence. We stop at a garage and I'm momentarily confused until I remember that Jesse works at his dad's station.

"Do you mind pulling it forward for me?" He gets out to lift the door and I slide over into the driver's seat. Once inside, he lowers the door, shutting out the world beyond these four walls.

I scoot over but only to the middle. "Not what you expected, huh?"

I'm not at all surprised. "I've come to expect anything after our field trip to the playground and the football field."

"When I wasn't on the football field, I was here with Earl. He was always teaching me something about engines."

I'm suddenly all nerves. I fidget, looking around, taking in his dad's garage. I'm procrastinating.

He rolls the ignition key and turns on the radio again. "Is this station all right with you?"

A soft love song is playing—an ideal mood-setter for the things I want to say to him. "Perfect."

"You're fidgeting." He reaches for my hand. "Are you that nervous about telling me?"

I stop twitching and shrug my shoulders. "No."

"You're a terrible liar."

"So I've been told."

I'm at half past the point of no return and the unknown of being with him no longer frightens me. I love him and I'm ready to shed the camouflage. I want to be completely exposed.

"Thank you for giving me the time I asked for. You didn't have to do that. You've been incredibly understanding and although it was unintentional, I know I've hurt you."

He squeezes his eyes tightly. I think he's bracing to hear what he's mistaken as a goodbye. I take his hand and bring it to my lips, placing a kiss on top. "You're so much more than I expected, even more than I dared hope for."

I lean over and press a light kiss upon his lips. "I feel myself … going under." It comes out as a whisper. "I'm drowning in my love for you. You're the only one I want."

A smile replaces the fear and worry on his face. "I was terrified you wouldn't take a chance on someone like me."

"It doesn't feel like taking a chance when it's right." I need to tell him the rest. "But I still have to break up with Forbes."

He puts his arm around me and I lower my head against his shoulder while he strokes my arm. "I want you to do it as soon as possible. I can't stand the thought of you being his for another minute."

"You can take me back to Dane's so I can do it now, but that means giving up this time together." I lift my face and kiss his stubbled chin. "I rather be here with you, but I'll do it if it's what you want."

I sit straighter and move my lips along his jawline until I reach that sensitive place on his neck below his ear. His kisses on me in the same spot pull me into a stupor. A groan escapes his lips and I'm certain we'll be staying right where we are. No way he's giving this up.

We're sitting side by side. The position isn't optimal for making out so we glide over until he's sitting in the middle of the cab. I turn and swing one leg over his body, climbing on top of him, my knees on each side of his hips. I'm desperate to feel his body pressed against mine.

He reaches beneath my dress and places a hand on each of my hips. He drags my groin against his, pressing his bulge against me. We do this same motion several times and I reach behind his neck to tighten our embrace. It feels like we can't get close enough.

His mouth abandons my lips and trails kisses down my neck, onto my chest. He tugs at the top of my dress and my black lace bra is exposed. He rakes his tongue upward through the middle of my cleavage and he's trembling beneath me.

I never went this far with Forbes in the eighteen months we were together, but being with Jesse is different. It feels right. But I'm not ready to be intimate with him, and we should be on the same page.

I lean back and cup his face with my hands, putting my thumbs on his lips. "I know I just crawled up here like I was going to devour you, but I can't have sex with you." Yet. "I'm sorry. I want to, but I'm a virgin and I'm not ready to change that."

He nods while my hands are still holding his face. "I know."

Everyone assumes I've been sleeping with Forbes because we've been together so long, so why would Jesse think differently? "How could you possibly know?"

"Forbes was bragging about how he was going to screw you the night of the bonfire. The only reason he would do that is because he'd never been with you."

He might not want me if I'm not going to sleep with him. "Does this change anything?"

"Sex isn't the reason I want you. I'd be with Gretchen if that's what I was after." He wouldn't even have to work for it with her.

I don't want to jump from one guy trying to get in my pants to another, so I feel like he needs fair warning. "I don't know when or if I'll be ready. You should know that up front."

He rubs his hands up and down my back. "This is enough. Just being with you is all I need."

His reassuring promise confirms how right this is between us. "I want more of this—touching and kissing. I love feeling you against me, but I don't want to be a tease so I need you to tell me if it's too much."

"You've told me up front to not expect sex. That's the opposite of a tease." He kisses me on the chest again. "I won't lie and say I don't want you because I really, really do, but your boundaries are clear and I respect them. If things get too heated, I'll tell you to back down and give me a minute."

He still wants to be with me without the expectation of sex—it's such a relief. My love for him grows because of it. "I don't deserve you."

He hugs me. "You're wrong. It's me who doesn't deserve you." He releases me and rests his head against the back of the truck's seat. His neck is completely exposed. I want to take full advantage so that's where I begin kissing him until he's breathless and trembling beneath me.

CHAPTER TWENTY-THREE

JESSE BOONE

D ON MY LEG AS I DRIVE TO HER HOUSE. I COVER HER HAND WITH MINE AND lace our fingers together, occasionally bringing her palm to my lips for a kiss. "Do you have to work tomorrow?"

"I work every Saturday. It's the only day I can get a full shift." I need every hour Earl will give me.

"Could I talk you into a date tomorrow night since we can't spend the day together?"

Does this girl not realize she could talk me into anything? "I could be persuaded."

This time it's her who brings my hand to her lips. "With a kiss, perhaps?"

"It's a good possibility." I laugh.

"Would you mind staying in? I want to cook for you." That's surprising.

I remember her saying she'd want me to meet her parents if we started dating. "Are you asking me to do the parent thing?"

"No. My mom and dad are out of town until Sunday evening, so it'll only be us. But we can go out and do something if you'd prefer. It's not a big deal."

I'm relieved she isn't asking me to spend time with her mom and dad. I'm not ready for that. "I'd love to come over, but I won't get off work until six."

"Could you be there around seven?"

An hour gives me time to get cleaned up. "Seven works for me."

Our goodbye is different when I take Claire home this time. It's more like our make-out session at the garage and I'm dangerously close to needing a minute to compose myself when she tells me it's a good idea for her to go.

Instead of walking around to get the door for her, I open mine and slide out. She exits behind me and gives me one last kiss before going inside for the night.

Once I'm home and in bed, I can't fall asleep. I can't stop thinking about my reality with Claire. It's far better than any dream I had. I replay the memory of her telling me she loves me and I have mixed feelings. I'm thrilled because she loves me but a relationship with her means I'll eventually be forced to come clean about my life. I can't hide my past from her forever and I'm terrified she'll see me for what I really am and realize she's too good for me.

My fear of losing Claire keeps me awake most of the night. I'm exhausted when the alarm screams but I get up for two reasons: Earl is counting on me to be there and it's my only remedy for empty-pocket syndrome.

Earl beats me to the garage today and is under an old Buick when I walk into the shop. "Mornin', Earl."

"Mornin' to you, lover boy." I knew I was going to catch hell from him about Claire. "You're late. Could you not drag yourself away from dreaming about your new girl?"

I look at the clock on the wall in the shop. "I'm not late. You just beat me here this morning, old man."

He glides out from under the car. "Things going good with your little lady?"

"Couldn't be better. She invited me over for dinner tonight—said she wants to cook for me."

Earl wipes his hands on an old rag. "Good. You can find out

early if she's wife material or not."

"I think it's a little early to be evaluating her for that."

He laughs. "Look, kiddo … it's never too early to evaluate a woman's ability to cook."

No one is preparing gourmet meals at my house. "I'm not used to getting anything more than a bowl of cereal so whatever Claire cooks will be fine by me."

"It doesn't mean she has skills just because she's asking you to eat her cooking. I once dated a woman who thought she was the best cook ever, but it was total shit."

I might need advice on what to do if Claire's cooking is bad. "How did you handle it?"

"I married her and had my mother teach her how to cook."

Oh. "I love Miss Hazel's food. I can't imagine her ever being an awful cook."

"I couldn't imagine myself marrying a woman who couldn't boil water—but I did—so if your girl can't rustle up a good meal, at least make sure she's teachable."

Earl always looks out for me so I guess this is his fatherly advice, even if it's coming way too early. "Teachable. I'll remember that."

Aside from the occasional inspection sticker, my day is filled mostly with oil changes, which is good. I'm less likely to drop a wrench on my face that way.

Earl lets me leave a little early since the afternoon is slow, so I go by the florist and pick up a bouquet before hurrying to the mall to buy a new shirt. I choose a light blue pullover for my first real date with Claire. It isn't a popular brand like the kids at East Franklin wear but the saleswoman said I had to get it because it matched my eyes perfectly. I hope Claire likes it too. The money I spent on it was supposed to go toward my truck.

After rushing to get ready, I make it to Claire's at seven on the dot. I knock nervously, flowers in hand. I feel silly and cliché.

She answers the door wearing a sexy little sundress and I swallow hard as I hold out the flowers. "Hope you like gerbera daisies." I couldn't afford the roses I wanted for her.

"I do, very much so. Thank you." She sniffs the flowers as she swings the door wide. "Come in. Dinner's almost ready."

She takes me to the kitchen and I study my surroundings as I follow her. Her house is even bigger than I thought and looks like something out of a magazine. Nothing seems out of place. It could possibly pass for a museum if not for the occasional family photo. "Your house is beautiful."

"Thanks. My mom is really into home decor. It's way too formal for my taste but it's the way she likes it."

We go into the kitchen and Claire tells me to relax at the bar while she finishes cooking. I sit on a stool as she ties an apron over the top of her sundress. I can't help but think she looks domestic—like she should be someone's sexy wife rather than a seventeen-year-old girl.

I can't cook for shit but I should offer to give her a hand. "Is there anything I can do?"

She looks amused. "Nah, I've got this. I've known my way around a kitchen for a long time."

She looks comfortable and confident as she whirls about in her apron. "I take it you enjoy cooking?"

"I do. I love to try new things. I mess up every once in a while but who doesn't?"

No one's ever shown me how to cook so I teach myself as I go, mostly learning from mistakes. "I mess up more than occasionally."

She bends over to peek in the oven and I watch her sundress climb the back of her thighs. "Maybe I can teach you."

I'd let her instruct me on anything. "I'm up for it anytime."

I convince my eyes to look away from her hemline just in time for her to not see me checking her out. I smile innocently while reminding myself of her boundaries.

I shouldn't torture myself by looking at her like that again.

"It's almost done." She places two plates on the counter and fills our glasses with ice. "Do you want a soft drink or sweet tea?"

"Water is fine with me. I don't make a habit of drinking soft drinks. You shouldn't, either. They're not good for you."

She whirls around to look at me. "You'll smoke cigarettes that give you cancer but you won't drink a soda?"

"I didn't say I never drank them. I said I don't make a habit of it. And by the way, I stopped smoking. I haven't had a cigarette since Tuesday morning, four very long days ago."

"What made you decide to quit?" She has to know she's my reason.

I want her to see what I'm willing to do to please her. "It's for you, princess."

She comes to me and puts her arms over my shoulders. "Thank you."

I take her face in my hands. "I'll do anything for you. That's how much you mean to me."

She puts her hands on top of mine. "I broke it off with Forbes today."

Thank God. "How'd that go?"

She steps away and looks at the floor. "Let's just say not well."

My heart speeds and my back stiffens. "Did he hurt you? I'll kill him if he touched a hair on your head."

"It was nothing like that. He did a lot of yelling. It was ugly." She nibbles her bottom lip. "He knows my parents are gone so I completely expect him to show up here tonight."

"Which means he'll see my truck here."

"Yeah, and he's going to have a total come apart. He really, really hates you."

"Well, I'm not in love with him, either. He can go crazy on me if he likes but he'd better not so much as look at you wrong or I will take him out." And I mean that. I won't let him hurt Claire.

The timer goes off on the oven and she gives me a quick kiss on the lips. "Let's not talk about him anymore. The lasagna is done and I'm ready to eat. Are you hungry?"

I haven't eaten a thing since lunch. "Starving."

"Good, because I have plenty."

She takes the lasagna out of the oven and plates two servings alongside salad and garlic bread. "You can take our drinks to the dining room if you'd like. I've already set the table so have a seat and I'll be there in a minute."

I go into the dining room and sit with extreme care. The formality of the room makes me nervous.

Claire comes in a moment later and places dinner on the table before lighting a couple of candles. "Bon appétit."

Her lasagna is fabulous. She passes the wife-material inspection by Earl's standards. "This is delicious. Who taught you to cook?"

"My mom but she typically cooks traditional. She's doesn't like to try new foods so I watch a lot of cooking shows. Sometimes it's good. Other times … not so much. But I'm learning. I kept it simple tonight. I didn't want to scare you off with something weird."

I don't think she could scare me off if she fed me live bear. "Thanks for the invite and going to the trouble of cooking for me. Everything's been perfect."

"The night isn't over." She flushes deep crimson before looking down at her plate.

"You're blushing."

She covers her face with her hands. "And you're pointing it out."

"Only because I'm intrigued about why."

She removes her hands from her face and tucks her hair behind her ears. "Later, okay?"

Curiosity is killing me but I agree to drop the subject for the time being. "Okay, but I won't forget."

We finish dinner and I volunteer to clean, but she only agrees to allow me to help. Once finished, we move into the living room and sit side by side on the couch. She flips through the channels and comes across a chick flick. "You want to watch this?"

I will for her. "We'll watch whatever suits your fancy. It's princess's choice since you cooked for me."

I point to her feet. "Here. Put your feet in my lap and I'll rub them for you."

She kicks off her sandals and spins around. I take her tiny feet in my large hands and begin massaging as we watch the movie. She occasionally makes a sound that can only be described as something between a sigh and a moan. I concentrate on everything in the room trying to not get turned on by her noises. I don't think she intends them to sound sexual, but the more I try to ignore it, the worse it gets. Before I know it, my hands are drifting from her feet to her lower legs.

I stroke from her ankles to her knees and down again, over and over. Her legs are soft and smooth against my palms and I ache to feel more of her, but I don't dare cross her bounds.

She removes her feet from my lap and I curse myself. I've pushed too far. "I'm sorry, princess. I shouldn't have …" She interrupts my apology by kissing my mouth urgently. She puts her hands in the back of my hair and presses my mouth hard against hers. A moment later, she falls back on the couch bringing me to lie on top of her. She squeezes me tightly and bends her knees so I'm tucked snugly between them. She brings her legs up and around my waist, pressing my groin against hers.

Oh hell. This is too much. I need a minute.

I break our kiss to tell her I can't go this far without taking it all the way and I see someone standing behind the couch ogling us. It takes a second for my brain to register what I'm seeing.

Forbes Henderson is watching me and Claire dry hump.

I shove the bottom of Claire's dress down. "What the hell are you doing in Claire's house?"

Claire bolts up from the couch. "How did you get in here?"

"God, Claire! You're screwing the Collinsville skank!" Forbes yells at the top of his lungs. "When did you decide to go slumming?"

"Get out, now!" she shouts.

Forbes fists his hair and slurs, "How can you be so stupid? He doesn't care about you. He's just screwing you to get to me."

He stumbles toward her but I block him and put my hand on his chest. "Whoa. You're drunk. You seriously need to back off."

He attempts to push me out of his way but only manages to stagger backward. "Shut up, skank. You don't belong here."

"Don't, Forbes," Claire says.

"Don't what? Remind him he's trash and not one of us?" he yells.

Claire crosses her arms over her chest. "We broke up and you have no right to come into my house uninvited."

"How do you think your parents will feel about you slumming with the trash?"

"Don't call him that!" she screams.

"I don't understand you, Claire. We've been together for a year and a half and you broke up with me so you could screw around with a nobody you've known a month."

She shakes her head. "You wouldn't understand, Forbes. And I'm afraid you never will."

"You're right. I'll never understand why you'd choose him over me." He takes a step toward her. "He'll never be able to give you the things you want or need."

"I want you out now!" she says.

I've had enough of this dickhead. "It's time for you to go."

I'm preparing to physically throw him out on his ass when there's a knock at the front door. Claire and I look at one another. This could be bad if he's brought reinforcements.

She peeks through the side glass and then opens the door. It's Cooper. "I thought I'd find him here. I tried to take his keys but he got away from me. I'll get him out of here."

Cooper goes into the living room and puts his arm around Forbes to guide him out. "Come on, buddy. You're coming with me."

He doesn't fight Cooper. I think the alcohol is close to rendering him helpless but he turns to me on the way out the door. "This isn't over by a long shot."

I go to Claire after they're gone and I hold her tightly because she needs to feel safe. We stay that way for a while but I eventually loosen my hold. She seems hesitant to let go. "I don't want to be alone tonight. Will you stay with me?"

CHAPTER TWENTY-FOUR

CLAIRE DEVERAUX

THE LOOK IN FORBES'S EYES WAS FERAL. I'VE NEVER SEEN HIM LIKE THAT. IT'S frightening and I'm unnerved by his ability to slip into my house unnoticed. I'm positive I locked the front door after letting Jesse in.

Another nerve-racking factor is my bold invitation for Jesse to spend the night alone with me in my house. I lift my head from his chest to gauge his response and see an expression I can't identify. "I'm sorry. I shouldn't have asked. Your parents will be expecting you home tonight."

His strong arms squeeze me tight and he strokes his hand down the back of my hair the way a parent comforts a child. "I'm staying. There's no way I'll leave you in this house alone after what just happened."

I don't tell him but I'm instantly relieved. "I know I locked the door after I let you in."

"Are there any keys hidden outside?" he asks.

"There's one but he doesn't know about it."

"It's probably wise to bring it in."

We go outside to retrieve the key from its hiding place. "It's been moved—he had to have used it to get in."

Jesse looks so angry. "That was a daring move. I think you should turn on the alarm as a precaution."

I can't believe Forbes went so far. What is wrong with him?

Jesse places two fingers under my chin and lifts my face so I'm looking at him. "Don't be scared. I'll be with you if he comes back. I won't let him hurt you."

I relax because I'm confident in Jesse's ability to protect me. "I don't think I could stay here tonight without you."

"Are we going to paint our nails and talk about boys at this slumber party?" he laughs.

I put my arms up over his shoulders. "I'd rather pick up where we were before the interruption." He doesn't look excited about that. "Did I do something wrong?"

"No, you were doing it exactly right and that's the problem."

"I don't understand."

"Making out like that is different for a guy. We get … worked up fast and it's hard to reel it back once it happens."

Oh.

"Things were too heated for me. I was about to tell you I needed a minute before I looked up and saw Forbes."

I drop my face and press it against his chest because I'm mortified. I've teased him past the point of his boundaries. "I'm sorry."

He takes my face in his hands, forcing me to look at him. "It's not your fault that you're too damn sexy for your own good." I can't stop my delight from spreading because I'm thrilled to hear him call me sexy.

"Aha! There it is—that smile I love so much," he says.

I grasp his hand and tug him toward the sofa. "Will you watch a movie with me if I promise to not assault you this time? You can choose since you're staying over to babysit me."

He opts to finish the movie we started earlier because he wants to please me and it's another reason to be crazy in love with him. How could I not love a guy who would voluntarily suffer through a chick flick?

I'm apprehensive about initiating physical contact with Jesse again so I let him make the moves. He puts his arm around me and pulls me close. It feels right to lean my head against him and relax my hand on his leg.

I HAVE no idea how long I'm out but I can't recall much of the movie when I wake. My neck is stiff from being cocked to the side for so long.

"Hello, sleeping beauty."

I stretch my neck a little more and hope his arm doesn't feel the way my neck does. "I'm sorry. I didn't mean to fall asleep on you. Is there even a remote possibility that you have a little circulation in your arm?"

He rolls his shoulder. "My arm's fine. But there's no way I'd complain it wasn't. I had entirely too much fun listening to the things you said while sleeping. You have some fairly interesting ideas about me."

Heat rushes to my face. "I don't want to know anything I said."

"Good call." He laughs.

I squeeze my eyes shut and try to recall what I was dreaming about.

"I'm pulling your leg, princess. You didn't say anything. You might have sighed a little but it was all completely innocent."

I'm relieved but I slap him on the leg. "I'll get you back for that."

"I love seeing your cheeks light up like that, which reminds me. What had you flaming at dinner?"

Oh God. I should've known he wouldn't forget. "I was thinking about something I wanted to ask you."

"I can't wait to hear what's so incredibly blush-worthy."

"What am I to you?" I whisper.

He fires back without hesitating, "What do you want to be to me?"

"I asked you first." I can't bring myself to put it out there.

"I only know what I want you to be."

"I need you to say it so it's clear."

"You're my only girl."

His only girl. "I like the sound of that."

I nestle back into my comfy spot. "Is princess sleepy?"

"Maybe. A handsome guy with the most magnificent pale blue eyes kept me awake last night. He told me he loved me and then kissed me for hours and hours and hours so I'm tired tonight."

"I didn't sleep much last night, either. This beautiful girl told me she loved me and then made out with me for hours and hours and hours."

"Then I think it's time to go to bed."

I get up from the couch but he doesn't move. "I think this couch will sleep better than my bed at home."

No way he's staying here all night on an entirely different floor. "I want you to stay upstairs with me."

"I don't think that's a good idea."

Who knows if we'll ever have this opportunity again? "I need you to be close to me. I want to feel you by my side when I fall asleep."

He reaches for my hands. "Did he scare you that bad?"

"This isn't about Forbes." It's about us taking advantage of this opportunity to be alone. He's silent so I know he needs more convincing. "Who knows when we'll have another chance to get this close?" I say.

He sighs. "If I agree to this, you can't get me all revved up like you did earlier. No wrapping your legs around me. No rubbing your body on me. A saint can only take so much so I make no promises to hold back if there's a next time." This is his warning. Don't go there if I'm not prepared to see it to the end.

"I'll be a good girl." I make the promise but it could be an empty one.

"That naughty grin on your face plants seeds of doubt in my mind."

I tug on his hands to get him up from the sofa. "Come."

He follows me upstairs and uses my brother's bathroom to get ready for bed while I ready myself in my bathroom. I brush my teeth and wash my face before changing into a tank with matching boxers. I brush my hair and tie it into a messy bun on top of my head.

I open the bathroom door and see a shirtless Jesse standing at the foot of my bed wearing a pair of my brother's knit pajama pants. I stop dead in my tracks because reality sets in. I'm about to crawl into bed with the hottest guy I've ever seen.

"Which side of the bed do you sleep on?" he asks

"All sides but I start out on the left side," I laugh. "I'm kind of a crazy sleeper. At least that's what I've been told. You can give me your opinion in the morning."

"Am I going to wake up in a headlock?" He's being funny and it helps break the tension.

"I won't say it's not a possibility per my family's comments."

He removes the throw pillows from my bed, tossing them into the chair in the corner. "You might have mentioned that in the disclaimer."

"You still would've agreed."

"Yeah, I know."

I stand frozen by my bathroom door but not because I'm scared of Jesse. I'm in awe of his body. His masculine beauty begs to be touched and I'm curious about what he'd say if I go back on my promise to be a good girl.

I shake my head, trying to clear those thoughts. "Did you find everything you needed in Ryan's bathroom?"

"I did, thanks."

He looks concerned when I don't make a move toward the bed. "Are you sure this is what you want?"

I nod because I'm rendered speechless by the anticipation of sharing a bed with this beautiful man tonight.

I walk to my side of the bed and we turn back the linens, climbing in together. I roll onto my side to face him and prop my head in my hand. My bedside lamp gives off a dim glow but it's enough to allow me a good look at him.

I examine his tattoo first. This is the first time I've had the opportunity to really look at it in its entirety. It extends much further into his shoulder and chest than I guessed. I trace its intricate detail with my fingertips.

He smiles as my fingers glide over his skin. "Why are you so fascinated by my ink? It's just a tattoo."

"I'm not fascinated. I just really like it—a lot. I love what it says about you."

"What exactly does it say about me?" he asks.

I trace a black curve with my finger. "That you don't care what anyone thinks. You're living for you, not everyone else or what they want for you."

"I think you're reading more into it. I really got it so the ladies would think I'm hot." He smirks.

I feel a pang of jealousy when I think of Jesse with another girl touching him this way. "Just how many girls have seen your whole tattoo?" I'm questioning him about girls seeing his tattoo, but what I'm really asking is an entirely different question.

"Don't go there, Claire. You won't like the answer." This is his way of warning me I won't be able to handle the truth. Maybe I can't. The thought of him sleeping with another girl makes me sick.

I'm debating if I'll push the issue when he puts his arm out for me. "Come here, babe."

I scoot closer and rest my head on his shoulder. "You're the only girl for me now. The others are in the past and that's where they'll stay."

I put my palm on his chest and stroke it back and forth across his muscular chest. "Is it okay for me to touch you like this?"

"Yeah. I like it. It's very relaxing."

I continue caressing his chest until his breathing becomes deep and steady. I roll away to turn off the light but he catches me by the wrist. "Don't go, princess." His voice is pleading.

"I'm only turning off the lamp. I'm not going anywhere."

I turn the switch and nestle back into my spot against Jesse. I swirl my fingertips up and down his chest and stomach, exploring his body. His chest quickly returns to rising and falling deeply, confirming he's back asleep, therefore ending any further wandering I have on my mind.

"Sweet dreams," I whisper, hoping any he has will be only of me.

CHAPTER TWENTY-FIVE

JESSE BOONE

I WAKE WITH CLAIRE BLISSFULLY BURROWED INTO ME AND IT'S A GIFT I DIDN'T think could be real. I bury my nose in her hair and inhale deeply, taking in her smell. I didn't notice last night but her bed smells just like her—sweet and floral with a hint of peach and cherry.

I'm lying with her draped across my body. I think about the way she stroked her hand over my chest rhythmically until I fell asleep and I can't think of a time in my life when I've been more relaxed and content.

I lift my head slightly and find our tangled legs intertwined with the bed sheet. One of her arms is stretched over my lower abdomen, dangerously close to the waist of my borrowed pajama pants. I lower my head to the pillow and close my eyes, trying to concentrate on anything other than the position we're in.

It doesn't work. I'm hard and I can't help it. It's biology.

Claire wakes a few minutes later and aggravates the situation by squirming against me as she stretches. I pull the sheet higher trying to camouflage the tent in my pants.

She lifts her face to look at me and smiles. Not a stitch of makeup on and she's still breathtakingly gorgeous.

I reach out and touch her face. "You are so damn beautiful."

"Can you stay with me every night because I'd love to wake up to this every morning." I wish.

"I doubt your parents will go for that." She doesn't disagree and I decide to tackle a topic I'll probably regret. "The things Forbes said about me are true. What do you think your parents will think of me?"

"Nothing he said was true." She sounds a little miffed.

It's time to get real about this. "If you were being honest with me and yourself, then you have to admit most of it is true. I don't fit in. I'm not like all of you. I don't have money and I damn sure don't come from a family like yours."

She sighs. "It doesn't matter to me and it won't matter to my parents, either. They are well off and they're friends with wealthy people, but they are kind and fair. They won't judge or dislike you because you don't come from a wealthy family."

I don't just not come from a wealthy family, I come from the bottom of the pond where the scum grows. The thought of sitting down with Claire's parents makes me want to run in the other direction. "I've told you I don't do the parent thing."

"You said that you're a part of my life now and so are they. I won't keep the two separate. No exceptions."

This is my fate—to meet the parents. "Do I have a deadline?"

"Can you come over next weekend? My dad won't be on call so they should be free. Maybe Saturday night?"

I'm conceding against my better judgment. "If I have to."

"You have to. Or you could stay today and meet them this afternoon. Your choice."

Even if I was willing, I can't. I have an appointment to see my little brothers at their foster parents' house today. "I have a family thing today."

"You never talk about your family."

I'm not ready to tell her truth. "There's not really much to say about them."

"When are you going to let me meet them?"

I dodge her question. "Why don't you let me make it through meeting your parents first? They're the ones who really matter. Then we'll go from there."

"Your family is important too. I want them to like me." God, she's so sweet. I hate lying to her.

I kiss her on the tip of her nose. "Who wouldn't love you?"

"Hold that thought." She gets up to the bathroom so I use the opportunity to go to her brother's. Being away from her for a few minutes helps alleviate the hard-on she gave me.

I brush my teeth with the new toothbrush and toothpaste Claire gave me last night, so I'm freshened up when I return.

She's already back in the bed so I climb in next to her. She snuggles up to me and I wrap my arm around her. Nothing in the world seems more perfect than this moment.

I look at Claire's nightstand clock and it's after eleven. I have less than two hours until my appointed visitation with Harley and Ozzy, so I need to go home and get ready. "I really want to stay in this bed with you all day but I have somewhere to be soon. I need to go."

"The family thing?"

"Yeah." At least I'm not lying about that. It does involve my family. "I have to be there at one but first I have to go home to get ready."

"I'll agree to let you go on one condition."

She's in a bartering mood. I can't wait to hear this. "And what's that?"

She lifts her brows. "Kiss me so good I won't be able to stop thinking about you for the rest of the day."

"Oh, I can do that," I say. We rise to our knees to meet in the middle of the bed.

My mouth lands on hers and she teases me, nipping at my bottom lip with her teeth before gently sucking it into her mouth. She has no idea what even her chaste kisses do to me.

She sits back on her bottom and I roll on top of her, taking control of our kiss but realize too late I'm not in command of my body. I have a yearning burning out of control. I kiss down her neck and argue with my mouth when it wants to go lower, but I lose the argument when my lips trail kisses down between her breasts. She gasps and drags her fingernails down my bare back.

I go lower and worship her body with my hands as I lift her shirt to kiss her stomach. She whimpers and wiggles beneath me and I realize I'm teasing her far worse than she did me last night.

I stop and she lifts her upper body, propping on her elbows. "What is it?"

"I'm sorry. I got carried away." We can't keep doing this. Stopping is brutal.

She falls back against the pillow and exhales deeply. "Ya think? You did that on purpose to teach me what it feels like to need a minute."

She isn't the only frustrated one. "I didn't mean to go that far. Really. In case you haven't noticed, I'm needing a minute here too, you know?"

I groan and collapse on the bed beside her, both of us on our backs staring at the ceiling in silence. When I look back at the clock, it's eleven thirty, well past time for me to go. "I have to go, princess. I can't be late."

"I know."

My folded clothes are on her dresser. I drop the pajama bottoms I borrowed and pull on my jeans while Claire watches me from her bed. "What?"

She's blushing again. "I wondered if you were a briefs or boxers man."

"And now you don't have to contemplate anymore."

"I sure don't."

I pull my shirt over my head and then sit on the edge of her bed to put on my shoes. She slides over and puts her arms around my waist, her head pressed against my back. "I love you."

I turn my head and whisper over my shoulder, "I love you too."

I grasp her hand around my waist and bring it to my lips for a kiss. "I gotta go, princess." She gets out of bed to walk me out the door. "Turn the alarm on when I'm gone."

"I'll be fine. My parents will be home soon. Don't worry."

"I know, but now it's my job to worry about you because you're my girl."

"I love it when you call me that." She hugs me one last time and I leave the girl I love and adore to go see the brothers I also love and adore.

I PULL up at the Stevens's house a few minutes before one and see Harley and Ozzy's faces pressed against the glass of the big window in the front of the house. The boys run toward me, calling my name, and meet me in the yard, nearing tackling me to the ground. I can't believe they're getting so big.

I stand on the lawn with a kid hanging on each leg and I hunker down to hug them. "Happy birthday, guys!"

"Did you bring us presents, Jess?" Ozzy's repetitively patting my shoulder to get my attention.

They know I do. I'm the only one who ever gives them anything. Twyla and Rita sure didn't. "Of course I have gifts for the birthday boys. You know I wouldn't forget."

"Where are they? I want mine now." Harley's so impatient.

"I know you're excited, but what do we say about patience?" I always have to remind him.

"A man who masters patience can master anything." The three of us say it together.

The Stevens seem like a nice family and I'm grateful for them providing Harley and Ozzy with a stable home, but I'll admit it irritates the shit out of me to have to ask permission to spend time with my own brothers. I'm the one who has parented them since their births four and five years ago.

"I need to talk to Mr. and Mrs. Stevens first, but if it's all right with them, I want to take you out for a little while."

The boys yank my arms, dragging me toward the house. "Ask them now 'cause I know they'll say yes."

I go in the house and spend a little time with my brothers' foster parents. They're very complimentary about the boys and their behavior. I ask permission to take them out for the afternoon and they agree to give me three hours.

I didn't know if Mr. and Mrs. Stevens would have a birthday cake for Harley and Ozzy, so I bought them a small one and put four candles on one side and five on the other. We sit at a picnic table in the park and I sing "Happy Birthday" before telling them to make a wish and blow out their candles.

"I wished for you to come live with us at Brian and Heather's house." That's just like Harley to tell his wish. He can never keep a secret.

"You're not supposed to tell anyone what you wished for or it won't come true," I tell him.

He shrugs his shoulders. "Ain't gonna come true no way so it don't matter."

These kids break my heart. "You never know."

Ozzy pipes in. "I'm not telling what my wish is 'cause I want it to come true."

I cut the cake and put a piece in front of Harley. He looks at the cake and then at Ozzy. "Don't get your hopes up."

I hate seeing Ozzy's hope snuffed out. "Sometimes hope is all you have and you don't have the right to take that away from him, Harley."

I pass a slice of cake to Ozzy and his face beams. "Chocolate. My favorite."

They finish their cake and open the gifts I brought. I didn't have a lot of extra money so it's a good thing it doesn't take expensive gifts to please them.

My time with the boys is too short but I return them to Brian and Heather when the three hours are up. That's when the worst part comes. They cry and beg me to not leave them. I promised to see them again soon.

I pull away, promising myself we'll be together again one day. I don't know how I'll pull it off, but I'll find a way.

CHAPTER TWENTY-SIX

CLAIRE DEVERAUX

I open my front door and Payton barges in. "Start from the beginning because I want to know everything. And don't you dare give me the spicy-edit version. I want to hear about some heat so give me the full monty."

"I'm crazy about him. Being with him is intense. I want to rip his clothes off and just … gah!" I fall back on the couch. I can't even articulate what I want to do to him.

I prop up on my elbows. "I know what people are going to think and say about us but I don't care. I honestly don't give a shit."

She snaps her fingers and waves them at me. "That's called love —the real and authentic kind. I know I said some harsh things about him. I'm sorry for judging him prematurely."

She hates Forbes so her approval really is an improvement. "I did as well, so don't feel bad."

She tucks her legs beneath her bottom, making herself comfortable for my tale. "Tell me all about last night."

"He spent the night." I can't control the squeal that escapes my mouth.

Payton's mouth is agape and she's silent … for a second. "No damn way. Did you play carpenter and let him nail you?"

She has such a way with words. "How romantic."

"You've not denied it," she says.

"No, we didn't play carpenter."

"Did you plan this spend-the-night ahead of time without telling me?" She sounds hurt.

Oh God. She doesn't know about Forbes breaking in. "No. The way it came about is a story all in itself."

She screeches in frustration. "What happened? You're killing me here."

I reiterate every detail and even she can't believe Forbes was so bold. But she brings up a good point I hadn't considered. Forbes may or may not have seen Jesse's truck outside my house. He was really drunk, so who knows? But he didn't know Jesse was here when he chose to come over, so what was he planning to do to me?

"You know I can't stand Forbes but you'll need to thank him for that stupid move. You couldn't have planned that whole scenario more perfectly if you'd tried." She's right. I'm not sure Jesse would've stayed if Forbes hadn't broken in.

"It was the best fourteen hours of my life."

"I know what would have made it better. I can't believe you slept next to him in your bed and didn't let him hit it. Who's urge meter was on the fritz—his or yours?"

There's nothing wrong with my sex drive department. "My urge meter is fully intact and the bulge he gets in his pants every time we make out proves his isn't on the fritz, either."

Her mouth forms an O. "You are so going to do him. I can tell."

I slap her leg. "Payton!"

"You were never like this with Henderson," she says.

It's true. I never once thought about sleeping with Forbes. "Things are different between me and Jesse. He does something to me that Forbes never could."

"I saw it the first day of school," she says. "He's your wonderwall."

"My what?"

"Wonderwall—the person you're in love with and think about all the time."

Oh. I guess he is. "I love him. I truly, madly, deeply love him."

"What about Mr. and Mrs. D.?"

I don't think it's a big deal. My parents aren't stuck up like Payton's. "He's coming to my house to meet them next weekend."

"He may be a bit of a culture shock for them but I think they'll be okay with your relationship once they get to know him and get past the whole sexy-convict appearance."

I hate when she says that. It sounds so judgmental. "You've got to stop saying that. He's not a convict. He's a law-abiding citizen. In fact, he plans on going to law school."

She looks surprised. "Whoa—was not expecting that."

"Me, either."

"That should score some points with your parents."

I don't want to consider the possibility of them disapproving. "I've had time to think it over and I've decided I won't give him up, even if they think he's not good enough or the wrong kind of guy for me."

We hear the door from the garage open and my mom calls my name.

"In here," I shout from the living room.

Mom comes into the living room and sits in the chair across from me and Payton. She's positively glowing. "You and Dad have a good time?"

She sits so properly with perfect posture even after driving for hours in the car. "It was fantastic. We both needed that getaway. We have to do that more often; I feel so refreshed."

I'm perfectly fine with them going away as much as they like so I can have more sleepovers with Jesse. "You should because you deserve it." I wink at Payton. "You and Dad need a break from all the chaos."

She tells us all about their refuge in the mountains while Dad unloads the car. When she finishes, she asks about my weekend. I debate telling her about Jesse. Maybe I should since I'm sure Mrs.

Henderson will be calling soon to talk about my breakup with Forbes.

Dad hasn't questioned me about Jesse since he saw us kissing at the hospital, but I'm positive he told Mom. It wouldn't be like him to keep that from her, though she hasn't said a word.

Payton's presence could be the ideal buffer for this conversation. "I broke up with Forbes while you were gone."

My mom leans back into the chair, positioning herself as she does when she's in counselor mode. "Would this breakup have anything to do with a certain young man you were seen kissing in the emergency room earlier this week?"

I knew my dad didn't keep it from her. "Yes and no. I didn't have girlfriend-type feelings for Forbes. He never made my heart race. I didn't know it was supposed to until I met Jesse."

"And Jesse makes it race?" she asks.

"He does."

"I have to admit I've been feeling a little left out since your dad has met Jesse and you haven't even mentioned his name to me."

I hadn't considered that. "I didn't know if we were getting together or not, but it's official now. I've asked him to come over next weekend if you and Dad are free. I'd like you to meet him."

"I think that will work but I need to check with your dad before we finalize anything." Oh God. Now I'm nervous. This is really happening.

"Is he cute?" Geez, is he ever! I think I want to have his babies just so my kids have a chance at inheriting his baby-blue eyes.

I giggle at my silly thought. "Mom, he's beautiful. He has the most captivating eyes I've ever seen."

"You're giddy and beaming just talking about him. I never saw you this way about Forbes."

I'm so glad to have my mom's support in breaking things off with Forbes. "I didn't know what your reaction would be."

"We love the Hendersons but we don't want you to date their son if you don't want to." Mom shrugs. "Forbes doesn't have the 'it factor' for you, but I can tell by the look on your face that this new guy certainly isn't lacking it."

Jesse certainly has the "it factor." He has the everything factor.

I get up from the couch and go to my Mom for a hug. "Thank you, Mom. You have no idea how much better I feel."

My dad walks in on our embrace. "Did you miss us that much?"

I go to my dad for a hug as well. I don't want him to feel left out. "I missed you too, big guy."

"Your daughter just told me she's broken up with Forbes and has a new guy in her life—just as you said. You were right."

My dad laughs. "Dee Dee, are you just now figuring out after all these years that I'm always right?"

I wait until my parents leave the room to start jumping with joy. "I can't believe how easy that was."

"You're really lucky your parents are cool. I wish mine were more like yours."

Payton has it rough, especially with her mom. She's a bitch. "I know. I have great parents—even better than I thought. Now I really can't wait for Jesse to meet them."

IT WENT JUST as I expected. Jesse and I were the talk all over school this week but I don't care. I no longer have to hide my feelings for him, so I proudly show him affection every opportunity I get, letting the world—and East Franklin High—know he's mine.

It's Saturday night—time for Jesse to meet my parents. I stand by the window in the living room watching for him. I pull the curtains back every few seconds looking for his truck. "Claire, you're going to jerk the drapes off the rods if you don't leave them alone."

"Sorry. I'm just excited." As well as anxious and nervous. "I really want you to like Jesse because he means a lot to me."

My mom smiles and gives me a reassuring hug. "Stop worrying. If you like him, I'm sure your dad and I will too."

I hear his loud truck out front and my heart beats a million miles a minute. "He's here. Go into the kitchen and let me bring him in there to meet you." The living room is so formal. I'm afraid it'll make him more nervous if he has to sit down with my parents in there.

"Kitchen it is." My mom laughs. I'm sure she thinks I'm being silly but she doesn't know Jesse the way I do.

"Where's Dad?" I panic.

"His office."

I straighten my dress and wait for the knock. I hear three thumps and casually open the door to find my boyfriend standing there looking not quite like my Jesse.

He's wearing a blue-and-white-checked, button-down shirt with the sleeves rolled to just below his elbows and khaki cargo pants. I bet he's never worn anything like this a day in his life.

I'm certain the longer sleeves are to hide his tattoos. My heart leaps because I know his choice of attire is an attempt to gain my parents' approval, but I never want him to pretend to be someone he's not. "Who are you and what have you done with my boyfriend?"

He holds out his hands and shrugs. "Does this pass inspection?"

I step outside the door and give him a quick kiss. "You always pass inspection." I run my finger over his mouth, wiping away the evidence of our kiss. "Are you ready for this?"

He swallows hard. "Ready as I'm ever gonna be, princess." He smiles but it doesn't reach his eyes, telling me he isn't so sure.

"Don't worry. You've got this." I give his hand a squeeze. "I love you so I'm confident they will too."

We hold hands as we walk inside my house. I feel like I'm dragging the sacrifice to the altar but everything will be fine in a minute.

Then we can both relax.

CHAPTER TWENTY-SEVEN

JESSE BOONE

I'm a coward. I want to turn tail and run but I don't because this isn't about me. I'm doing this to make Claire happy. If doing so requires that I meet her parents, then there's no debate. I will do this for her.

I want to win the Deverauxs' approval. Nothing would suck more than Claire's parents disliking me, so I'm wearing this goofy-ass shirt to cover my tattoos. I'm not hiding them because I'm ashamed. They could become fixated on the ink and fail to see I'm a great guy. I want them to see me tonight, not some inked-up punk ass.

My girl loops her arm through mine and squeezes my bicep as we walk through the foyer. "You didn't have to hide them."

I cup my hand over hers. "I didn't want them to miss the forest for the trees."

She nods. "I get it, but please know it isn't necessary."

Her father is coming into the living room as we enter. "Dad, you remember meeting Jesse at the hospital?"

"I certainly do. It's good to see you again, Jesse."

Claire releases my arm so I can shake her father's hand. "It's good to see you again, Dr. Deveraux."

"I was at the game last night. You're quite the quarterback."

"It was a good game."

He gestures toward the couch and I take that as his cue to sit. "You're an extremely talented young man. College scouts will be looking at you for certain."

I relax a little when I see he wants to talk football. That's a breeze. "I'm hoping for a scholarship."

"You shouldn't worry. I'm confident you'll get plenty of offers if you continue to play like you did last night."

Claire elbows me. "I tell him that all the time."

"What are your plans after high school besides playing college football?"

I think this is the father test. He's checking to see if I'm considering my future—one worthy of his daughter. "I'd like to study law—preferably become a prosecutor."

"I think you have a bright future ahead of you, Jesse. Your family must be proud." I don't say anything because I don't want to tell a lie I can't fix later.

"Claire, honey, why don't you take Jesse to the kitchen to meet your mother? I'll join you in a minute. I need to finish something in my office."

Claire is beaming because she's so happy with the way things are going.

We go toward the kitchen and she reaches for my hand. "My dad was the one who had me a little nervous but that went super. My mom will be an ace in the hole. She's very excited about meeting you."

Mrs. Deveraux is checking the bread in the oven. Claire gives me a wink before she notices us. "Mom, I want you to meet someone." Her mother straightens and turns around. "This is Jesse Boone. Jesse, this is my mom, Deandra Deveraux."

No. No. No. This can't be happening. Her name is Wesson, not Deveraux.

I feel my heart take off so hard, I hear the pounding in my ears.

I'm numb as I stare in disbelief at my psych counselor, the woman that knows my every secret.

Claire squeezes my hand. "Is something wrong? You look like you've seen a ghost."

A ghost would've been more preferable. "No, I'm fine."

Deandra is wearing a face of shock, much like mine, but she manages to reel it in. "It's very nice to meet you, Jesse. Claire has told us some great things about you."

She steps over and pulls out a barstool, the one I occupied the night Claire cooked for me. Oh shit. The same night I slept in her daughter's bed. "Come sit and drink something. You look pale. Claire, pour some tea for Jesse."

I sit in shock. Claire is Deandra's daughter. What are the odds? The one girl in the world I love with all my heart is the daughter of the woman who knows my deepest, darkest secrets.

Deandra's pretending she doesn't know me. I don't understand why she isn't screaming for me to get out of her house since she knows what I am and where I come from.

Claire is across the room getting ice from the refrigerator when Deandra whispers, "I can't tell her anything—not even that you're my patient. I'm bound ethically."

Claire returns with a drink. "Maybe this'll make you feel better."

The dizziness has passed. I take a big gulp but I still can't say anything.

"Better?" Claire asks.

I look up from the floor and nod. "Absolutely."

The oven timer goes off and Deandra takes the bread out. She looks at me. "I hope you feel well enough to stay for dinner. We're having grilled tuna steaks."

"Tuna steak isn't weird," Claire assures me. "Remember, I told you she isn't brave enough to try weird."

My mind buzzes. I want to run so I can get away from the woman who knows more about me than any mother should about her daughter's new boyfriend.

Claire and Deandra finish cooking dinner and prepare the table while I sit at the bar deciding how I think this might play out. Were we really going to sit through dinner pretending we didn't know one another?

I go over her words in my head. She's ethically bound and can't tell Claire anything. That means she expects me to.

Like everything in my life, this is a hopeless situation. There is no way she'll allow Claire and I to be together because she knows I sell drugs—not of my own accord—but ultimately that doesn't matter in the eyes of a mother.

Being with me is dangerous and she knows it.

"Everything's ready. Go tell your dad to come on." There it is— her way of getting me alone so she can tell me how I'm going to end things with her daughter.

Claire leaves the kitchen and I wait for her instructions. "I won't tell Claire you're my patient, but you will end this relationship with her. I don't care what you tell her. She will not be tied up in the things you are involved in and we both know what I'm referring to."

She's right. I shouldn't have become involved with a nice girl like Claire. She had no idea what she was getting herself into with me. "I didn't know she was your daughter."

"I believe you but it doesn't change things. I can't allow you to be a part of her life."

Our private conversation ends when Claire and Dr. Deveraux come into the kitchen. "Smells good, Dee Dee."

We're at the dining table and Deandra pretends everything is normal. "Claire and my husband tell me you're quite the quarterback. Warren says the college scouts will be buzzing all around East Franklin to get a look at you."

If she can pretend, so can I. "I sure hope so. I'm counting on a football scholarship."

"You must have good grades if you're in the advanced placement humanities class with Claire," Dr. Deveraux says. "What about an academic scholarship as well?"

"I have a 4.0 GPA, so it's a definite possibility."

Claire stops eating and looks at me. "I didn't know that."

I shrug. "It never came up."

"Looks like Brad isn't my only competition for valedictorian. I may need to step up my game." Claire laughs.

We finish dinner and Claire tells her parents we're going up to her room. I know that can't be okay with Deandra.

"You know the policy. Keep the door open," her dad calls out.

I follow Claire to her room and she sits next to me on the edge of her bed. She leans over and bumps her shoulder against mine. "Do you still feel bad? You were really quiet at dinner."

"Just nervous, I guess." I don't like lying to my princess.

My princess. I won't be calling her that for much longer.

She laces her finger through mine. "You shouldn't be nervous. They loved you, so all of this nervousness is for nothing."

My mind wanders. How am I going to tell the girl I love that we're over?

She twists toward me and shoves me back onto the bed, crawling over me while kissing my neck. "Whoa, Claire. Your parents are right downstairs," I whisper.

She looks down at me smiling. "You never call me Claire so you must really be nervous. Don't worry about them. Their bedroom is downstairs and they never come up here."

She goes back to kissing my neck and begins unbuttoning my shirt. I give her hand a gentle nudge. "I don't feel right about doing this. What if one of them comes up and we don't hear them? They would freak if they walked in on us like this."

"You're right. I'm sorry I'm making you feel uncomfortable but you have this way of making me want you so badly." She takes my hand and sucks one of my fingers into her mouth. "I'm not always in control with you. I'm sorry you're often forced to wrangle me."

Oh shit.

The whole Deandra thing has thrown me for a loop and I have some serious thinking to do. "I think I'm gonna go."

"No. Please don't. I'm sorry. I'll be good. I promise." She climbs off and reaches for the remote on her nightstand. "We can watch television. See? It will be very innocent."

Even if I stay, I wouldn't be with her because my mind is somewhere else pondering how to end things with the one who means everything to me.

"I'm sorry. I have to go." I don't offer an explanation.

I can see her disappointment and it kills me. I'm sick with the thought of hurting her, but I have things to sort out and being with her in this house isn't the way to get it done.

She grasps my arm as I get up from the bed. "Can I see you tomorrow?"

That's not a good idea. "I have a lot to do so I don't think it'll work out."

She looks hurt but it's only a prelude to the pain I'm going to cause her when she finds out everything.

She follows me as I go down the stairs to the front door. We pass through the living room where her parents are and I continue the game Deandra and I are playing. "It was nice meeting you both. Thank you for dinner, Mrs. Deveraux. I really enjoyed it."

Lies. Lies. Lies. I hate the way they make me feel.

"Thank you for coming, Jesse. It was very nice to see you again," Dr. Deveraux says.

"I hope you'll come back," Deandra says. That's laying it on a little thick.

I don't give Claire the chance to walk me to my truck. I wouldn't be able to stand kissing her goodbye. "I'll see you on Monday."

I leave her standing at her front door as she watches me drive away. I'm certain she's confused about how the night could've begun so well and then ended so abruptly.

I'm driving home and all I can think of are the things I told Deandra. Shit! She knows nearly every detail of my pathetic life so I can't blame her for not allowing Claire to be with me. It's useless. Trying to persuade her otherwise isn't even an option.

Now, I must choose how I'll break my princess's heart.

CHAPTER TWENTY-EIGHT

CLAIRE DEVERAUX

WHY DOES IT FEEL LIKE JESSE JUST WALKED OUT OF MY LIFE?

I want to cry. Things started out so perfectly with Dad and then everything seemed to suddenly go wrong when he met Mom. I'm certain I didn't imagine it and I'm going to get down to the bottom of it.

I hurry inside and go to the living room to confront my mom. "Something is wrong with Jesse. He was fine when he got here. He and Dad hit it off great, and then I watched him change the second he came into the kitchen to meet you."

I let my unspoken accusation linger as I watch her face for any sign of an explanation, but she looks blank. Unfeeling, even. "What happened, Mom? I don't understand."

"I don't think he felt well. He probably wanted to leave earlier, but stayed for dinner out of courtesy." Bullshit.

My dad interjects to support my observation. "He didn't seem ill when I spoke with him. I thought he seemed glad to be here, maybe a little nervous, but he was fine. I too saw a change in him so I have to agree with Claire. Something happened from the time I spoke with him until I saw him again at dinner."

My mother looks uneasy. "I didn't do anything to Jesse."

"Did you say something to him when I walked out of the room?"

"We spoke when you went to get your father." I know my mom well enough to recognize when she's choosing her words carefully.

"What did you say to him?"

She shuts her eyes and lifts her head toward the ceiling. "I can't tell you."

"There's only one reason you would say you can't tell me what you talked about with someone." She doesn't reply and my stomach drops to my feet. "Omigod, Mom. Jesse is your patient!"

"I can neither confirm nor deny that." She's using her clinical voice.

"Mom! You're the reason he clammed up all of a sudden. He's never going to come back," I scream. "Because of you!"

"I have an oath and I can't tell you anything."

Tears well in my eyes. "This isn't about your stupid oath. It's about me and Jesse. I love him, Mom, and I need you to make this right. You have to tell him you don't hold anything he has told you against him and he is welcome in our home."

"This is a very delicate situation," my dad says.

My mom won't even look at me.

I need to talk to Jesse right now but I have no idea where he is or where he lives.

I run to my bedroom to find my phone. I call Jesse but he doesn't answer, and I'm not surprised. I send a text saying I need to talk to him but I don't expect a response after that shitstorm.

I call Dane, the only person I can think of who might know where Jesse lives. "Hey, it's Claire. I'm trying to find Jesse and I don't know where he lives. Do you have any idea?"

"I've never been to his house. We always hang out at my place but the things he's mentioned makes me think he lives on the south side of the county. I have a hunch he lives in that trailer park on the county line but I've never asked because I didn't want to embarrass him."

I'd never had a reason to explore the south side so I'm not familiar with the area at all. "I don't know where you're talking about. Would you take me?"

He doesn't answer immediately. "Are you sure that's a good idea? If he wanted you at his house, he would've taken you there."

"He wouldn't have taken me there if he's embarrassed and I want him to know he shouldn't be."

I can tell he doesn't want to upset his friend but he finally concedes. "It may not even be where he lives. The only thing we could do is drive out that way and look for his truck."

I'm willing to try anything. "I really want you to take me. I need to see him, Dane."

I send up a prayer and wait for his answer. "I'll pick you up in fifteen minutes."

I breathe a sigh of relief. "Thank you so much."

"Well, I'm not taking the blame if we find him and he's mad as hell about you showing up at his place without an invite," he warns.

I wouldn't dream of it. "I promise I'll take all the blame."

Dane pulls into my driveway and I race out the door before he has a chance to get out of his car. I get in and tell him again how grateful I am for his help.

He drives in the direction of where he suspects Jesse lives. I've never been out this way but there's a distinct difference in the housing the farther south we get. We leave the grand two-stories behind and head into what most of my friends would call a ghetto.

I hope Dane is wrong about where Jesse lives but if he isn't, it doesn't matter. I love him and I don't care what kind of house he lives in or if he doesn't have money.

Dane turns into a place where mobile homes are lined with only enough room for a built-on porch and a couple of cars in between. We search for Jesse's truck as we slowly drive through, but there isn't a sign of it. My hopes fade.

Dane sees the disappointment on my face. "I guess I was either wrong about this being the place or he didn't come home after he left your house."

I begin to cry out of desperation. I have to find Jesse so we can straighten things out. "Thanks for trying."

"Please don't cry. I'm sure it's not as bad as you think. I know that Jesse is crazy about you, so I'm sure you'll work it out." He tries to comfort me but it's of little consequence.

"I don't know if we will. It's pretty serious." I sob as we continue the search for Jesse's truck.

After two hours of riding around, I finally give up and tell Dane he can take me home. I try one last time to call Jesse but it goes straight to voicemail. "Jesse, please call me. I really need to talk to you … Please. I love you."

SUNDAY PASSES without a word from Jesse and I'm terrified he's decided things aren't going to work between us. I don't sleep well for a second night, so I get up while it's still dark to get ready for school.

I wait in humanities and I'm short of breath when he finally comes through the door. This is it—the moment of truth.

He puts his backpack down and takes the seat next to me. "Hey, princess."

Hearing him call me that makes me feel a little more at ease. "Hey, you." I look down at my notebook and doodle a few hearts as I build the courage to ask what happened after he left my house. "You didn't return my calls or texts."

He rakes his hand over his face and I notice the stubble. "I'm sorry. I know you're probably confused about what's going on, but we don't have time to get into it before class. Will you meet me after practice so we can talk?"

I don't know what this means. "Of course. Do you want me to meet you by your truck?"

"That'll work." He doesn't look at me. I take that as a bad sign.

What feels like years later, I hang out by his truck, my stomach tying itself in knots. I dread this conversation because I'm certain it's going to be near impossible to convince him that his sessions with my mom aren't relevant to our relationship.

He looks exhausted as he walks toward me and I wonder if it's from practice or if he's as sleep deprived as I am. "You look really tired. Is now a bad time for us to talk? We can wait if you want."

I'm a coward. I don't want to hear this.

He shakes his head. "No. I need to do this."

Oh God. He's about to break up with me.

My heart picks up speed as I get in the truck with him. Once inside, he puts his head against the seat and closes his eyes. He looks like he's wrestling internally.

"You said you needed to do this. What does that mean?" I brace myself for the worst.

He inhales deeply before slowly blowing out through pursed lips. "I don't want to see you anymore. I pretended I was in love with you because I wanted to take you from Forbes. I thought I could get in your pants but since you shut me down on that, there's really no need to continue on with this."

"I don't believe you. This is about something else."

"Just because you don't believe it doesn't mean it isn't true." He's staring out the window because he can't look into my eyes as he denies his love for me.

"You're lying. You can't even look at me when you say it."

He whirls around and grabs my jaw so we're face to face. "Every time you teased me, I was thinking about how I was going to be with Gretchen when I got away from you. That's right, Claire. I've been screwing her all along."

Tears are welling, threatening to spill from my eyes.

I was wrong. This isn't about my mom at all. I'm only a game to him and we were never real. He doesn't love me because if he did, he wouldn't use Gretchen to hurt me.

Tears spill and roll down my cheeks, collecting against his hand where he's still holding my jaw.

This isn't what I expected and I'm completely unprepared for it. I jerk away and silently stare at his eyes for a moment before I open the passenger door. I stumble when my feet are on the ground, my legs threatening to give way.

I leave his passenger door open and run toward the refuge of my car. I have no idea how long I sit there staring blankly at my steering wheel, but there isn't a car remaining in the lot when I finally come to my senses.

I look where Jesse's truck was parked and it's gone as well.

I gather myself enough to drive home but all I feel is numb. I park in my usual spot but I have no memory of how I got there. It's like an out-of-body experience.

I walk into the house and my mom says something that sounds like static. I ignore her. I climb the stairs to my bedroom and throw myself across my bed, the one I shared with Jesse not so long ago.

My mom knocks and eases my door open. "Can I come in?"

I don't answer and she mistakes my silence as an invitation. She sits next to me on the bed and strokes my hair the way she did when I was a little girl. "Things didn't go well today?"

"Jesse broke up with me." I still can't believe it, even as I hear myself say the words.

"Do you want to talk about it?" she asks.

I'm not ready because the cut is too fresh and deep. "I can't right now."

"You know you can tell me anything when you decide you're ready. I'm always here for you." She pulls me close and hugs me tightly.

"You shouldn't be shocked if I'm never ready."

CHAPTER TWENTY-NINE

JESSE BOONE

CLAIRE IS MY EVERYTHING. SO I'M BACK TO HAVING NOTHING SINCE SHE'S NO longer mine.

Seeing her go was like one of those bad dreams where she slips from my grasp in slow motion and all I can do is watch. It was brutal but the worst was the look on her face when I told her I didn't love her. That's the darkest lie to ever leave my lips.

One look at her face—that's all it takes for me to be certain she believed my deception. I couldn't be more devastated about losing her but it's necessary if she's to believe I don't love her. Otherwise, she won't let me go.

I need to talk to someone. I would normally turn to Deandra for something like this but she's a no-go.

Not only have I lost my girl, I no longer have the only other person in the world I can open up to. That's not great. Sometimes talking to Deandra was the only thing getting me by when things got bad.

Dane. He's the only person I can consider talking to.

He answers the door and is still wearing his sweaty clothes from practice. Perfect. "I need you to come out and run with me."

He looks at me like I'm crazy. "You are out of your mind. My ass is dragging and yours should be too. Why in the world would you want to run after the workout we just had?"

"Because I need to talk and you're the only friend I have."

"Talking doesn't involve running."

Running doesn't require me to look at him as I talk. It'll make this less ... uncomfortable since what I'm about to say isn't something you'd sit down to discuss over tea. "You coming or not?"

He sighs deeply. "Hell, I guess."

We start running and I can't find the words to begin this tale. How do I own up to all the things going on in my life?

"I'm giving you one block to do your talking so you'd better get started."

"I broke up with Claire."

"Why? You love her." I recognize confusion in his voice.

"I love her with all my heart but there are things she doesn't know—bad things that will ruin the way she feels about me."

"Shouldn't that be her decision?"

"I'm no good for her. Hell, I'm no good for anyone. It's only a matter of time before she figures it out on her own."

"A chickenshit—that's what you are. You're scared and letting her go so you don't have to take a chance. You think that's easier than getting hurt."

"That's not true. I'm saving her from a shitload of pain."

"You're lying to yourself if you believe that and I wouldn't be much of a friend if I didn't call you out on it. Claire knows you don't come from money and she doesn't care. She was so upset on Saturday night that she had me drive her around for over two hours looking for you because you wouldn't man up and take her calls."

"You don't get it."

"You love her. She loves you. What's not to get?"

There isn't a way to make him understand without telling him what's going on. "I come from a place with people in it that you can't begin to imagine because that kind of ugliness doesn't exist in your world."

"Your family? How are they so different?"

It's been too long since I've opened up about my life and I feel like I'll snap if I don't tell someone. "I grew up seeing my mom deal drugs for money. I was ten the first time she made me sell."

He stops running and stares at me but I look away. I can't have eye contact when I tell him the rest. "One of her buyers came into our trailer last summer and killed her right in front of me because he thought she was ripping him off." I shrug. "And she probably was. He turned the gun on me and fired until he thought I was dead. That's how I got the scar on my shoulder, not from surgery."

It was scary as hell for me but I can't even begin to imagine what it was like for Harley and Ozzy. "My two little brothers were hiding in a closet in their bedroom. They were in the middle of that shit with bullets flying because of my sorry-ass mom."

He knows my past but now it's time to reveal my present, which isn't any more promising. "I live with my grandmother—the same one who taught my mom how to sell. She's forcing me to deal in exchange for a roof over my head. My brothers are in foster care and I'm trying to figure out how to get them back, so don't you dare tell me I took the easy way out. With everything I've been through, leaving Claire is still the hardest thing I've ever done."

"You can tell her what's happening," he says.

My life is beyond humiliating but at least I have the good sense to be ashamed. "I don't want anyone to know—especially Claire."

"I won't tell anyone, but you can't keep selling drugs, dude. You could go to jail." As if I don't know that.

I feel the need to defend myself. "I need a place to live so I don't have a choice right now."

I still haven't gotten to the best part of the story. "There's more and it gets worse. I was referred to a psych counselor for post-traumatic stress disorder after I was shot."

"No. Say it isn't so." He's starting to get the whole picture now.

"Yep. Claire's mother is my counselor and she knows everything about me. When I say everything, I mean it literally."

"Dayum, that's too bad."

That's the understatement of the year. "I wanted to die when I walked into her house on Saturday night."

"How did she react when she saw you?" he asks.

"She pretended we didn't know each other but she was sure to tell me to break it off with Claire when she got me alone." And I can't blame her for that.

"I'm sorry. I know how much you love Claire but right now, you need to worry about how to get away from your grandmother."

I think about it constantly but to no avail. "I don't have anywhere to go and I can't afford an apartment."

"We'll talk to my parents. They'll let you stay with us."

"I can't do that." I won't allow my troubles to become the Wickhams' problem. "I only have to live there until graduation and then I'll be free. I can get a full-time job and find my own place until fall semester starts. I'll live on campus after that."

"What happens if you get busted and go to jail in the meantime?" he asks.

"I'll be careful." It's one of the few things I'm good at.

I'M NOT ready to face Claire, so I don't go to school on Tuesday. Because it was so easy to not face her on Tuesday, I don't go on Wednesday, either. I show up on Thursday but only because I'm afraid I won't be allowed to play football on Friday night if I cut class more than two days.

I wait until the tardy bell rings before I go to calculus because I'd rather take the tardy than be confronted by Payton. I keep my eye on the clock, watching the time so I can bolt as soon as the bell rings.

In humanities, I dread the moment Claire will walk into class. I'm not sure I can handle seeing her face but I don't have a choice. It's inevitable.

The bell rings and she's yet to show up.

"I'm glad to see you've recovered from being sick," Mrs. Tanner says. "Whatever put you and Claire out of school this week must've been pretty bad. It looks like she isn't going to make it today, either. Have you spoken to her to see if she's doing better?"

This wasn't an illness I'd be recovering from anytime soon. "No, ma'am. I haven't."

She looks confused. "I hope she's all right."

If she's feeling anything like me, then she isn't.

I suffer through the hour and make a second attempt to avoid Payton when I get to history, but I'm not so lucky this time around. "I'm going to give you fifteen seconds to give me an explanation before I go postal on your ass."

I look down at my notebook because I'm afraid she might see what I'm trying to hide from her. "I don't have to explain anything to you."

She slams her hand on the desk, calling everyone's attention to us. "Uh, yeah … you do. I encouraged Claire to pursue a relationship with you because you convinced me you loved her. So you owe me an explanation."

I need her off my trail. "I played you and her—pretty well, I might add. It was always about taking her from Forbes so I could hand her back all used up."

It feels like she's staring right through me. "I don't believe you."

"It doesn't matter to me what you believe." I laugh.

"The grimace that accompanies a lie always tells the truth." Who knew Payton could be so philosophical?

Mr. Buckley ends our showdown when he begins class and I couldn't be more relieved. This girl is too perceptive for her own good. If I'm not careful, she'll crack this case wide open.

CHAPTER THIRTY

CLAIRE DEVERAUX

I'M SURPRISED MY MOM LET ME CUT SCHOOL FOR THREE DAYS. SHE KNOWS HOW hurt I am but it's Friday morning and she's decided enough is enough. She's been telling me that I can't avoid life—or Jesse— forever, and I have to return to school. She's right but that doesn't mean I don't dread seeing him.

I'm afraid I'll take one look at his baby blues and completely lose it.

My mom flipped on my bright light fifteen minutes ago but I pulled the covers over my head, promising her I'd get up in a few minutes. But I didn't. Instead, I'm lying in bed thinking about the things Payton told me when she called after school yesterday. She insists that her conversation with Jesse was off—that he seemed awfully affected for some asshole using me to get back at Forbes.

She's wrong.

The whole school must be laughing their asses off at how stupid I am. I bet they think I got exactly what I deserved for dumping Forbes to go out with Jesse. It's humiliating but I tell myself I did nothing wrong except follow my heart for the first time in my life.

Wow. Look what a disaster that turned out to be.

My mom knocks on my door. "Claire, you're going to be late."

I groan and drag myself out of bed while she watches, her way of ensuring I don't crawl back under the covers to feel sorry for myself.

I go into my bathroom and turn on my favorite playlist before getting into the shower. I stand under the falling water wishing it had the ability to wash away the events of the last few weeks—including Jesse. I wish I'd never met him.

"Stronger" begins playing. I've listened to it a thousand times but never truly heard the lyrics until this moment. I'm clearly not the only person in the world who has ever felt this pain given this song's lyrics. So why have I spent the last three days thinking the only solution for my heartache was to lie down and die?

I'm not over just because Jesse Boone chooses to be out of my life.

He's the one who should be ashamed of what he did—not me.

This pain won't kill me. If anything, I'll draw strength from it. And I won't go to school looking like hell today, either.

I have a surge of strength I've not felt in days. I'm excited to face reality and show everyone I can stand a little taller and a little prouder.

I apply a little extra makeup, hoping to hide the signs of what the last few days have left under my eyes. I choose one of my sassiest dresses and pair it with boots. One look in the mirror, and I feel confident. Who could look at me dressed like this and think I'm not over Jesse Boone?

After homeroom, I meet up with Payton at our lockers. "Well, someone looks quite well after not leaving her bed for three days."

I laugh. "It takes more than the likes of Jesse Boone to ruin me."

"That's my girl." Payton hugs me. "It's past time to file him under 'forget this shit.'"

"I wish I hadn't skipped school for three days like a wuss, but it's too late to change that now." I finish digging in my locker for my Spanish book and turn just in time to see Jesse walking toward calculus. He's ignoring me. "The only thing I can do is show everyone how unaffected I am by him."

"Omigod. You have no idea how glad I am to hear that. I was not looking forward to being all sympathetic and shit … but I still score friend points because I was prepared to do it, right?"

Payton does a shit job of being sympathetic. "You still get your friend points."

"Are you prepared for second period with him?" she asks.

"Absotively." I've got this. Even if I cave on the inside, no one will know. There isn't anyone who can put on a better front than Claire Deveraux. I'm the master.

I enter Mrs. Tanner's class and confidently sit in my normal seat next to Jesse. I refuse to give him the satisfaction of knowing how much he's hurt me.

"Claire, I'm glad to see you back in class," Mrs. Tanner says. "I was worried you were quite ill."

I shrug. "It was just little pesky bug I'm happy to be rid of. I'm very much over it now."

Jesse doesn't even glance in my direction as I boldly stare at him.

Mrs. Tanner doesn't give us a partner assignment today and I'm disappointed about that. I had every intention of proving I was over what happened between us, but I get no satisfaction because Jesse ignores me—in every way.

I'm sitting behind him and Gretchen in physics and notice they act nothing like a couple, but I guess they wouldn't since they're only sleeping together. Seeing them together reminds me of the things Jesse told me and my mind begins to imagine all the things he left out. I bet the two of them were laughing behind my back the whole time.

My instinct is to cry but I suck it up and sit a little straighter, holding my head high as I stare straight ahead. I pray Mrs. Bishop starts talking soon and holds my interest enough to end this torment.

FOUR WEEKS and Many Tears Later

The days run together as I masquerade through life. I pretend Jesse never hurt me—that what happened between us was an insane, momentary lapse of judgment on my part. I have everyone convinced but I can't win over the one who matters most—myself.

I've fallen back into my relationship with Forbes because it's familiar and safe. I thought he would make me forget about the one who broke my heart but instead he's become a constant reminder.

They say time heals all wounds. That's total shit. The harder I work to forget him, the more impossible it becomes to stop loving him.

The Wickhams are over tonight for the first time since my breakup with Jesse and I'm sitting across from Dane at the dining room table. He and I haven't talked much since the incident because he's best friends with the asshole.

My mind wanders to the place it always does and I'm curious to know if Dane knew about Jesse's plan to use me. I'll hate him too if I find out he sat back and allowed it to happen. "I need to talk to you for a minute. Go outside with me?"

He doesn't look at all surprised by my request. "Sure."

We go out by the pool and sit on the patio. "I'm surprised you haven't cornered me before now."

At least he doesn't insult me by pretending he doesn't know what this is about.

"Did you know he was using me?"

He exhales a deep breath. "There's so much more to this than you know."

I don't understand what that means. "Then tell me."

"You have the right to know everything but it's not my story to share. Jesse has to be the one to tell you."

"Tell me what?" I plead. "Please, Dane. If there's something I should hear, you have to tell me."

"Shit! He's either going to really hate me or really love me for what I'm about to do."

He's so mercurial.

"I can't tell you everything—that's for him to do—but I assure you that he didn't use you. Well … maybe he did a little in the beginning but never the way you think he did. Jesse loves you with all his heart and soul, but the boy has serious shit going on in his life."

I'm more confused than ever now.

"That's all I can say. He has to be the one to tell you the rest of his story."

It's hard for me to believe Jesse loves me after the way he ended things. "How do you know he loves me?"

"He told me he did. He came to my house after he broke up with you and told me everything. He's miserable without you, even if he acts like he's not."

He said he was screwing Gretchen behind my back. No way he loves me if he was doing that. "What about the penivore?"

"He lied. He's never been with her." Dane shoves his hands through his hair. "Oh man, he's gonna kill me for telling you this stuff."

"He'll never know you told me anything. I promise."

"What are you going to do?" he asks.

"I have no idea." But it's going to be good, whatever it is.

CHAPTER THIRTY-ONE

JESSE BOONE

THE LAST FOUR WEEKS HAVE BEEN A TOTAL BLUR WITH ONE EXCEPTION—I MISS Claire like crazy. I'm miserable without my princess. Watching her go back to Forbes has nearly killed me. The only thing worse than seeing her with him is the way she seems so unaffected by our separation. Her smile and laughter never escape my attention, and I admit it hurts to know she's picked up and moved on so quickly while I remain stagnant in my misery without her.

Football's the only thing that brings me any kind of peace. It requires enough concentration to temporarily get Claire off my mind.

It's Friday night and I'm standing on the sideline while my teammates play defense. We're so far ahead that the other team doesn't have a chance at making a comeback, so everyone has already started celebrating our victory.

Dane stands next to me. "Everyone's going out to Harrison's to celebrate after the game. You up for it?"

That's where Claire and I snuck into the woods to be together. It was the first time we admitted there was something between us, and I can't stand the thought of being there without her. "I don't think so."

"Why not?"

If he'd use his brain, he wouldn't ask such a stupid question. "You know why not."

"I don't get you, man." I guess he wouldn't since he's never been in love. "It won't kill you to have a little fun. You might actually enjoy it."

"I have to be at work early in the morning." It's a lame excuse.

"You're telling me you're going home so you can go to bed?"

"Rita's out of town on a pharmaceutical run so I'll have the place to myself. I plan to take full advantage." No drunks. No parties. Uninterrupted sleep. It's a luxury I rarely get.

"You're going to miss out on a lot of fun. You might even find a girl you like besides Claire."

Not possible. "I'll pass."

"You never know until you try."

He doesn't get it. I love Claire. There's no one else for me. End of story.

We win the game and go into the field house to change. I decide to hang out on the bench a few extra minutes because I don't want to see Claire and Forbes together after the game. He rubs that shit in my face more than I like.

I overhear a dozen different conversations about Harrison's place but one coming from the other side of the lockers catches my attention. "Claire isn't coming to Harrison's. She says she doesn't feel good, so I guess that means it's boys' night out."

What a douche canoe. He's happy about being rid of Claire instead of being concerned about the reason she isn't feeling well.

"You gonna give it to Gretchen again since your girl won't be around?" That's Cooper's voice. Is he talking to Forbes?

"Shut the hell up, dude. Don't be saying that shit out loud in here. Anyone could hear you." That was definitely Forbes. That dickhead is cheating with Gretchen behind Claire's back.

I hope the penivore is enjoying her victory. She couldn't convince me to screw her so she went for who she could get.

I feel a bit of satisfaction knowing Forbes won't be with Claire tonight but I don't like the idea of him cheating on her. I have no idea how their relationship has evolved in the last few weeks, but I find myself sick with wanting to know if she's given herself to him.

I will kill him if he's double-dipping.

The more I think about how far Claire has gone with Forbes, the more disgruntled I become.

I wait until I'm certain Forbes and Cooper are gone before leaving the field house. I don't want them to know I overheard their conversation.

I pull into the drive at Rita's and find the yard empty of cars. It's a welcome sight. I'm long overdue some time without Rita and her horde.

I go into the trailer and turn on some music before getting into the shower. I let the water run over me until there isn't one drop of hot water remaining, which doesn't take long. The water heater is on its last leg.

I dry off and wrap a towel around my waist. Who knew I could enjoying the freedom of being alone this much?

I go into the living room and I'm startled to see I'm not alone at all. A petite, auburn-haired girl sits on the edge of the couch in my grandmother's rundown trailer.

Something so beautiful clearly doesn't belong here.

I feel ill seeing her in this dump I call home. "What are you doing here?"

"I want to talk. I have things to say."

How did she come to be here? No one knows where I live. "How did you find me?"

She clasps her hands on her lap. "I followed you home after the game. Please, don't be angry."

Forbes said she was sick. "I thought you weren't feeling well."

"That's what I told Forbes so I could get away."

"So, you're back to that place—lying to your boyfriend so you can sneak away to go slumming with the skank."

"We wouldn't be at that place if you hadn't broken up with me."

I don't want to but I can hurt her again if it means keeping her away from this life. "It wasn't a real breakup because we were never a real couple."

She places her hand over her heart. "The pain I feel right here tells me every day that it's real, and I won't believe otherwise."

Now isn't the time to cave. "Your mistake."

She shakes her head. "Our relationship may have started out as a game to show Forbes what you could take from him, but it turned into so much more."

"Then I guess the joke's on me."

"You ended us because you were scared."

"Scared of what?" I laugh.

"Me finding out the truth about you."

"I'm a son of a bitch who used you. That's the only truth about me."

"It's not—not by a long shot."

She gets up from the couch and walks toward me. She waves her hands around. "I don't care about any of this. And it doesn't matter if you're seeing my mother for counseling because you have problems."

She's standing in front of me and grasps my jaw in her hand, just as I did to her the day we broke up. "It's your turn to listen to me. I know who Jesse Boone is and I love the person you are. I see all of this and I choose to be here with you. We belong together. I know it and you do too."

I'm surprised to learn that she knows about me seeing Deandra. "You don't know everything about me."

"Because you haven't allowed me to know."

It's time to end this and there's only one sure-fire way: the truth. "Everything you think you know about me is a lie."

"Nothing you say will change the way I feel about you."

We'll see about that. "Can you love a liar?"

"We've established that you've lied to me, so you'll need to do better than that."

"I have a criminal record."

She looks unfazed. "Keep going. You're not there yet."

"Is it your life's aspiration to fall in love with a drug dealer?" She's quiet so I have her attention now. The iron is hot so it's time to strike. "You want the truth even if it hurts?"

"I can take the truth. It's the lies that kill me."

"I'll do you a favor and give you the short version. I grew up with an addict for a mother. She was also a drug dealer and a whore so I have no idea who my father is." I point to my shoulder. "This isn't from surgery. I got it this summer when a buyer came into our trailer and shot me after he killed my mother in front of me. He thought I was dead—and I would have been if my two little brothers hiding in the closet hadn't come out after he left and called for help. They were put into the foster care system but because I'm eighteen, I was turned away so I struck a deal with my grandmother. I sell her dope and she gives me a place to stay."

Claire's silent so I guess my plan's working. "I don't want to be like this, but it's who I am and it won't be changing any time soon, princess."

"I don't care. I love you."

She needs to understand that this goes beyond the present. "I have things on my plate that no eighteen-year-old should have to worry about. I have a lot to figure out—like how I'll get Ozzy and Harley out of foster care. I'm going to be responsible for raising two little kids so being with me means taking on my problems. That's unfair to you."

"I'd rather have you with your problems than not have you at all."

There is no shining future with me. Why can she not see that? "The only place I'll take you is down."

"Then we'll go down together."

No. "That's not what I want for you."

"Because you love me."

"God help me, I do."

She's still standing close, searching my face. I swallow hard and she reaches out to touch my scar. She runs her fingers over it with the softest touch before leaning forward to place a kiss on it. I shut my eyes, squeezing them tightly as I relish the feel of her lips against my skin.

It's been too long since I've felt her.

She looks up at me. "I want to make all the bad things go away."

"I wish you could, but my demons aren't going to disappear. That's why we can't be together. I won't make you a part of this."

"I'm already part of this because you're in my heart."

I shake my head. "No! I won't let you be my fault."

She grabs my face, imprisoning me. "We can make this work."

I pull her hands from my face. "No, we can't. Your mother knows everything about me. She won't allow us to be together."

"It's not her decision," she whispers. She stretches onto her tiptoes and kisses me while running her fingers up the back of my neck and into my wet hair. A whimper escapes her mouth when I run my tongue over her lips. She squeezes me tightly, bringing my body hard against hers. Our kiss escalates and she walks backward, taking me with her toward the hall.

"What are you doing?" I ask, but the only answer I get is her tugging me down the hallway toward the bedrooms.

She stops at the first door. "Is this one yours?"

I nod because my head is too fuzzy to answer.

She leaves me standing in the doorway when she walks into my bedroom, waiting for me to join her.

She makes it so easy to forget about reality.

I can only think of having her back in my arms where she belongs when I cross the floor to close the distance between us. My mouth is on hers in an instant and my hands are under her dress, sliding inside the back of her panties to grasp her bare cheeks.

Claire glides her hands down my back and gasps when she realizes the towel around my waist has dropped to the floor. She drops her face and the top of her head is pressed against my chest.

The girl is checking things out down there.

Her hands come around my hips and she presses the flat of her palms against my upper thighs. She grates her nails up each side of my groin. I groan and jerk in response. "Hells bells, Claire."

She steps back and reaches for the hem of her dress, pulling it up and over her head. She tosses it onto my bed. "Don't stop this time."

She's wearing matching black lace panties and bra. "You're so damn beautiful."

I reach for her, taking her in my arms again. Her skin feels like fire against mine.

We fall onto my bed and she brings her bent legs around my waist. The only thing separating us when I press against her is lace. Her hips meet mine and we're rocking in rhythm together. "Make love to me, Jesse."

I want to. Bad. But this isn't what she deserves. "Your first time should happen somewhere special—not in a trailer park on the south side."

She kisses my chin. "It's special because it'll be with you."

"You can't take it back once it's done. I don't want you to ever look back on me as a regret."

She rubs her finger over my bottom lip. "Stop basing your idea of perfect on what everyone else says it should be. You are the only thing I need to make this perfect."

She came here to wear me down and she's doing a mighty fine job of it.

She arches and reaches behind her back to unfasten her bra before sliding the straps down her arms. She holds the cups in place for a moment and then pulls them away, baring her breasts to me.

She takes my hand and brings it to her chest between the two mounds. I slide it over, cupping one in my hand while rubbing my thumb over her nipple. She moans before rising onto her knees and swinging a leg over so she's straddling me. I grasp her hips and guide her up and down as she grinds against me.

A moment later, she moves to her back and pulls me down on top of her. I'm kissing her neck, migrating lower. I rake my tongue over one of her nipples and she shudders. I move to the other and do the same, getting a similar reaction. "Oh. That feels good."

Her knees are bent and widened, allowing my body to nestle between her thighs. I'm kissing her mouth again when she grasps my face. "I want you to think of me every time you lie in this bed and remember how good it felt when I gave myself to you for the first time."

Whoa. This is happening.

"Are you sure?"

"Never more sure of anything in my life."

I lean across her and she playfully sucks my nipple as I'm getting my wallet from the plastic crate next to my bed. I remove a condom and open it, rolling it on and squeezing the tip to ensure no air is inside.

I hook my fingers into the sides of her panties and she lifts her bottom as I slide them down her legs. I lower myself and nestle back between her legs, my erection pressed against her. "You know it'll hurt a little."

"I've heard." She looks terrified but I don't want this to be a frightening experience for her.

I've never been with a virgin so I don't know the best way to make it better for her. "I want this to feel good for you, so I'll go slow and be gentle." She's so tense. It's going to hurt more like that. "Baby, relax."

"Okay." She inhales a deep breath and blows it out slowly as her loosens her grip on me. "I love you, Jesse."

"I love you too." And I do. I adore this girl lying beneath me. I would do anything to make her world turn.

Her eyes are squeezed tight as I slowly push inside her. It doesn't feel different at first but then there's a little give, like maybe something is tearing. She gasps in pain and digs her nails into the skin of my back.

I become motionless because I'm hurting her. I've never caused a girl pain by doing this. They've always liked it. "I'm sorry. Do you want me to quit?"

She opens her eyes and holds my face with her hands. She stretches her neck to kiss me. "No. Don't stop." She relaxes beneath me. "Still go slow, though. Give me a minute to get used to it."

I'll have to go slow if she needs a whole minute to prepare before we do the real thing.

I move in and out of her slowly and she lies motionless. "Feel okay?"

"Yeah. The ache is going away." She's lifting her hips to meet my slow thrusts so we must be beyond the bad part. "It feels good now."

She tightens her legs around me but not in response to pain. She's enjoying it. I pick up speed and we get into a rhythm.

I want her first time to be unforgettable, not just a little pain and then movement she manages to tolerate. I want her to have an explosive orgasm and I know this probably isn't going to do it for her, so I push my hand down to our union and stroke her body just above. She jerks in response and I'm rewarded with her moan.

"Something's happening," she squeaks out.

I rub my fingers up and down while grinding my hips into her. "It'll feel so good if you just let it happen. Promise."

And then she does.

THAT WAS INTENSE.

We're lying side by side and her head is on my chest. Our legs are tangled and I'm stroking my hand up and down her arm. "Was it okay for you?"

"Are you kidding me? I don't have anything to compare it to, but that was so far beyond okay." She stretches to kiss the scar on my shoulder. "I really want to do that again soon."

"I can go along with that."

She giggles and a strange look comes over her face. She sits up and lifts the sheet. She looks back at me, blushing. "I'm bleeding on your bed."

I knew she hadn't been with anyone else but I feel something I can't describe seeing the proof that I'm the first to ever be inside her. I grasp her arm and pull her to me for a kiss. "I don't care."

I push the sheet away and turn to get out of bed. "I need to get rid of this."

She smiles, still blushing. Will she ever stop doing that? I hope not.

I remove the condom and tie it up, tossing it into the trash. I'm going back to bed when there's a fierce pounding at the front door. "Stay here. Don't come out no matter what. Got it?"

She nods as I pull on a T-shirt and flannel pants.

I open the door and it's as I suspect. One of Rita's customers. He's rubbing his arms and stutters out, "I need to see Rita."

"She's not here and won't be back for a couple of days."

I can see he's having withdrawal symptoms, so I'm guessing he's one of her heroin buyers. "I need a fix real bad."

I'm not doing this with Claire in the house. "I can't help you, man."

I swing the door to close it and he rams his shoulder into it. "You just think you're not gonna help me. I know Rita's got a stash somewhere in this house."

We struggle at the door. He's trying to push his way in as I'm shoving him out, punching my fist into his face. "Get the hell out of here."

He's suddenly screaming and rubbing his eyes, so I push him out and slam the door shut before locking it. What the hell was that?

Claire's dressed and standing behind me holding her keyring, a small can of pepper spray dangling from it. "Are you all right?"

"Fine." I'm short with her because I'm pissed off. I told her to stay in my bedroom and not come out because of a potential situation exactly like this. "Can you not do as you're told?"

She could've been hurt—or worse. Addicts are crazy as hell when they're in withdrawals, so this serves as just another wake-up call to remind me why we should never be together.

I look out the window and watch the man get into his car and leave. I grab Claire by the arm once he's out of sight and open the front door. I lead her to her car and open the door. "You've got to go and I don't want you to ever come back."

CHAPTER THIRTY-TWO

CLAIRE DEVERAUX

I KNOW THAT DIDN'T JUST HAPPEN.

I can't bear to lose him again. I won't survive it a second time.

I sit in my car staring in disbelief. How can I have him back for only a few minutes before he slips from my grasp again?

This isn't over.

I get out of my car and stomp up the deck attached to his house. I turn the knob on the front door but it's locked. I knock and call for Jesse, but he doesn't answer. I pound harder on the door and raise my voice. "Jesse, let me in so we can talk about this."

I beat on the door and the fear of reality sets in. He's turning me away again. Tears come to the surface and roll down my face as I beat my palm against the door and scream. "Jesse! Please! I know we can make this work because I love you."

He doesn't answer so I slide down the door like a lunatic and sit against it. I beat on the door for the next hour and cry in desperation but he ignores me.

A gust of wind blows in, bringing rain with it, and I sit until I'm soaked to the bone. I pound on the door another hour and call out for him until my voice is hoarse and I can scream no more.

Having no other choice, I give up and drive home. It's one o'clock in the morning when I walk through the door, soaking wet.

My mother is waiting for me in the living room. "You look awful. But I guess you should since you're supposed to be sick."

I don't say anything. "Forbes called to check on you. I told him you were asleep. Where have you been?"

I could lie and avoid the whole confrontation but I'm ready to get everything out into the open. "I was with Jesse."

I can see by the look on her face that she's displeased.

"Come sit with me." I fall into the chair across from her. "You are my daughter and I love you wholeheartedly."

"I know you do."

"What I'm about to tell you goes against everything I stand for as a counselor, but you're more important than any oath I've taken." She slides to the edge of her seat and clasps her hands on her knees. "I know you think you love Jesse, but that's because he isn't who you think he is. That boy's dangerous and no good for you. He'll only hurt you."

"I know what he does for his grandmother but it's not because he wants to. I know everything and it doesn't change how much I love him. I still want to be with him."

She shakes her head. "Jesse is a nice boy living in some very unfortunate circumstances. He's endured more than any kid should. It's a miracle he's still alive but I won't allow you to become part of his life. His world is dangerous."

She's making me furious. "You don't get to decide who I love."

"Jesse is smart and he knows your place isn't with him."

"He's only living there until graduation. After that, everything will be different."

"You aren't dating a boy who sells drugs. End of discussion."

"He's never had anyone dependable in his life and look how he's turned out. He's super smart and talented. He's going to make something of himself. He won't always be like this. It's temporary."

"You aren't having anything else to do with him."

I feel a screaming tantrum coming on. "I'm eighteen! You can't stop me from being with him!"

I run up the stairs to my room and slam the door. I'm glad she doesn't come up after me to try to change my mind. Any efforts would be in vain. I'm not giving up until Jesse is back with me.

MY MOM TAKES my keys and doesn't allow me out of the house for the rest of the weekend. It's a smart move on her part because Jesse's place is exactly where I'd have gone.

Since I was homebound all weekend, I look forward to school on Monday. I pray Jesse doesn't skip. I'm dying to see him.

My muscles are tense, jaw clenched, as I sit in my car waiting for him. I know what I have to do.

I see him pull into the parking lot so I scurry out of my car. I knock on his passenger side window before he comes to a complete stop. He hesitates. I think he's weighing the pros and cons of letting me in his truck. After a moment, he leans over to unlock the door and I jump in before he can protest.

We sit in awkward silence for a minute and I stare at my hands in my lap. "I'm sorry about Friday night. I shouldn't have come into your house without permission. I guess that makes me no better than Forbes. And I'm sorry I went crazy on you ... afterward."

I tack on afterward so he'll be forced to think about the beautiful intimacy we shared.

I look over at Jesse and he's staring out the window. "I wish my circumstances were different but there's no way to change any of it right now." He looks at me. "I love you with all my heart, but we can't be together while I'm in the middle of this shit. You'll end up hurt—or worse—and I'd never be able to live with myself if something happened to you."

"I'm not afraid."

"If I'm forced to decide between being with you or keeping you safe, I'll choose your safety every time." He raps his hand against the steering wheel twice, with his next words. "Every. Time."

"Nothing is going to happen to me," I tell him.

"Friday night was an eye-opener for me. I can't stand to even consider the possibility of what might have happened to you if that man had gotten past me."

I'm not helpless. "I think I did a pretty good job of defending both of us. Do I need to remind you I'm the one who pepper sprayed him?"

"Do I need to remind you that the only reason you had to do that is because you were with me? In case you've forgotten, it was a crazed addict, just like that guy who came into my house and attacked me and my mom." He reaches across the seat, grabs my hand, and squeezes it. "I would never forgive myself if … " His voice cracks and he doesn't finish his thought.

I'm desperate to maintain any form of contact so I slide across the seat and take his face in my hands. I love holding him this way. "Please don't cut yourself off from me. If I can't be with you the way I want, I'll take whatever I can get."

He wrinkles his brow. "Are you saying you want to be friends if we can't be a couple?"

I close my eyes and press my forehead to his. "I am if it's all you can give me for the time being."

He shakes his head. "I don't know."

I can't stand the torment of going back to pretending he doesn't exist, but even worse is him ignoring me. "Do you really want to go back to the way we've been for the last month?"

He puts his hands on top of mine. "I don't want to go back to anything that means we can't be together, but that isn't what's safest for you." He sighs. "I guess we can try it but I think you should stay with Forbes. It'll be harder to control myself with you if you're single."

That's just ridiculous. "Forbes isn't the one I love. I don't want to be his girlfriend."

"I think we're setting ourselves up for failure as friends if there's no accountability." I want to fail at being friends.

I feel nauseated by the thought of seeing him with another girl. "Are you going to be with someone else?"

"No. It's not safe for anyone to be with me but more so, I don't want anyone but you."

I want him to be happy but I'm glad he won't be with another girl. "It isn't fair. You shouldn't have to watch me with Forbes."

"It's the complete opposite of what you think. I'm actually being selfish by telling you to stay with him because I know you don't love him. If you were with someone else, I would be worrying the whole time that I was standing on the sideline watching you fall in love."

"So, this is it?" The question is painful.

He lets go of me and the loss of his touch is like a painful withdrawal. "This is it. Friends from this point on."

I look around the parking lot and then at my watch. "We're tardy."

"I know. But I don't care."

I look around again. The parking lot is full of cars but their occupants are long gone. "A little late or a little more late. The tardy is the same."

He grins. "What are you getting at, princess?"

My heart rejoices when he calls me that. It feels like old times.

I scoot to the middle of the cab until we're so close, air can barely separate us. "I need a proper goodbye if we're only friends from this point on."

"I don't think that's a good idea. It'll start something we've clearly decided should end."

"You decided it should end," I remind him. "I'm going along with it but I'm not letting you go until I get my closure. I'm entitled to that much."

I tilt my face toward his, taking the kiss I want and deserve. I tease him for a moment, placing a light kiss against his mouth before sucking on his bottom lip, tugging it. I prolong the playfulness of our kiss another minute but he groans and it sends me into orbit. I love this stubborn-ass boy with all my heart, and I know he'll never allow himself to be like this with me again so I'm desperate to make the most of it.

I turn to get on my knees and climb over to straddle him. I hold him tightly because I'm afraid he's going to push me away but he doesn't. Instead, he reaches beneath my dress and pulls my hips hard against him as he presses his groin into mine. I reach for the button on his jeans. "One last time," I whisper.

He reaches to help me unfasten his jeans—at least that's what I think—but I realize I'm wrong. He grasps my hand firmly. I know what's coming. He's going to make me stop so I kiss him down his neck to convince him to keep going.

"Claire, we can't have sex in the school parking lot."

I know it's crazy and risky but that's how bad I want him. "The hell we can't."

He grabs my shoulders and gently pushes me so I'm forced to look at him. "We aren't doing this at school. Anyone could walk by and see."

I'm desperate to hold on to this moment. "Then take me to your house or get a hotel room."

He's going to tell me no. Tears are building so I cover my face. My chest heaves from the sudden sobs. "I just want to be with you again, Jesse. I don't care where."

I open my eyes and he's crying as well. His tears shatter me. "I know. I want that so badly but we can't."

I sit straddled on top of him and we hold on for dear life as we mourn our loss.

I'm not sure how long we're like that when he tells me we have to go.

He's right—always the voice of reason—but I squeeze a little tighter. "Give me one more minute—just one more—and then I'll let go."

He gives me five and I cherish each one like it's the last I'll ever have with him. For all I know, it could be.

CHAPTER THIRTY-THREE

JESSE BOONE

IT'S RIDICULOUS TO THINK CLAIRE AND I CAN HAVE A GOODBYE KISS THAT doesn't turn into … that. The physical attraction we share is crazy. I agreed to her goodbye kiss knowing it would be intense but never dreamed we would end up crying in each other's arms like we'd never meet again.

We stand side by side at the office window waiting for our tardy slips and she allows her fingers to graze mine, sending tingles all over my body. I thought it was an accident until she does it a second time. I look at her and silently mouth, "Stop."

She smiles mischievously but then looks as though she might cry again. Her eyes are swollen and bloodshot. They've never been greener and she's beautiful because I know the tears she's shed are for me, for the loss of us.

She grazes my hand a third time. I look around for prying eyes but find none so I grab her hand and bring it to my lips for a kiss. She smiles and I promise myself we'll do better on this friend thing tomorrow. Today, I just want to make her happy.

We get our slips from the office and walk toward our first-period classes. We come upon my classroom first. "See you in humanities."

I look at my watch to see how late we are. Yikes, first period is almost over. "Yeah, pretty soon it looks like."

"Good." I stand at the door and watch her go down the hall. She turns to see if I'm still there and smiles.

We're being ridiculous—like two teenagers in love—because that's what we are. The absurd part isn't how we stand around grazing hands or the way we watch one another, hoping no one will notice. The ludicrous part is that we can't be two carefree teenagers in love.

We meet one another on the way to humanities and Claire loops her arm through mine. Her touch sends my heart galloping. She pulls away a moment later. I'm guessing realization set in. It's strange that we were so close only a half-hour ago and now we can't even touch.

We're in class a couple minutes when Mrs. Tanner announces we'll be spending class time in the library today. We walk there silently and then stop to look at one another as our classmates disperse.

"Do we go with tradition or choose a new table?" she asks.

We both know the safer thing—but that doesn't mean it's what we'll choose.

I don't feel like sharing Claire today. I want her all to myself. "Today's been filled with enough surprises. Why don't we stick to what we're used to? I think we do great work without distraction."

She smiles. "I couldn't agree more."

Yes. We will definitely need to do better tomorrow.

We're sitting at our table and she leans forward to get something out of her backpack. I watch the way her hair falls forward, forming a curtain to hide her face. It's the way it looks when she's on top of me, leaning in for a kiss.

She sees me watching her and smiles. "What?"

I shouldn't. It'll only stir trouble but I'm powerless to stop myself. "The way your hair falls as you lean over—it reminds me of the way it looks when you're on top of me. It rushes forward and falls against my face and chest. It always tickles and sends tingles all over my body."

"Hearing you say that sends tingles all over mine right now."

"I'm sorry." I shouldn't have thought it and I damn sure shouldn't have said it. "We can't say things like that anymore if we're only friends."

"We might be able to control saying it, but I don't think we can stop thinking it."

Third period is a little more friend-friendly since we don't sit together, but it's the same as always. I fight not looking her way. Of course, I'm weak and give in. Each time I do, she's looking straight ahead listening to Mr. Buckley and I wonder how she's finding this so much easier than me. The fourth time I steal a glance at her, she turns my way and I feel satisfaction in her desire to look at me as well.

The dynamics are strange. We never got to toy with a friendship because we jumped head first into a romantic relationship, so it's nice to see Claire in an entirely different light.

I'm changing out for practice when Coach calls me into his office. He never does that, so it catches me a little off guard.

I go to his office and stand, waiting for an invitation to enter. "Come in, Jesse, and shut the door."

I do as he asks before I sit in the chair. Interactions like these always make me nervous; it usually means something is wrong.

"I have fantastic news. I got a call from Doug Stanton today. Do you know who that is?"

Uh, yeah. Everyone knows Doug Stanton, the coach at UT. "Yes, sir."

"Doug's interested in you. He's heard about your talent and wants to come watch you play." My heart takes off like a helicopter. This is the first step to getting out from under Rita. "It's early in the season for anyone to be contacting me about you, but I think he wants to get a jump-start before anyone else has a chance. He's coming to next week's game."

The first thing I want to do is tell Claire—my friend. "Wow.

State is my first choice." It isn't far from Harley and Ozzy and the team has a great football program under Stanton.

"This is it, Jesse—the beginning of the rest of your football career. Places like UT are where you get noticed by the pros. You've got the potential to take it all the way."

I've never considered playing professional football. Until recently, I didn't have a chance at being discovered by anyone since I was stuck on a team at Collinsville with a loser coach.

It's best if no one knows about this, especially Forbes. "I don't want anyone to know."

"Why not?" he asks.

I decided to tell him the why but not the who. "Not everyone will be happy about this. I think it's best if no one has a heads-up in case they try to ruin it for me."

"You've been a team player by not saying anything, but I know who'd be interested in ruining this opportunity. I've had my eye on Forbes since the day you rode off the field in that ambulance. I've been his coach for too many years to not know him and his ways. That little shit doesn't have me hoodwinked."

Wow. Okay.

He nods toward the door. "Get your ass out there and practice so you'll be ready to bring your best for Stanton."

"Sure thing, Coach." I stop at the door and look back. "Thanks for everything. You have no idea how this could change my life."

"Nothing will be the same for you if this goes through, and I couldn't be prouder about having a hand in it."

I'm on the field for practice when I see Claire across the way. I'm eager to tell her about my good news but not because she's my friend. It's because I love her.

We can label our relationship whatever we want but things aren't different—with one exception. I'll hold her at arm's-length to keep her safe. Anything closer is a risk to Claire and that's not something I'm willing to chance.

CHAPTER THIRTY-FOUR

CLAIRE DEVERAUX

I WANT TO KNOW WHAT HAD JESSE SMILING SO MUCH BUT I'M AFRAID TO PUSH the friend envelope too far. I'm afraid he'll withdraw all contact if I act like more than a pal, and that's something I can't risk. Friendly contact is better than none at all.

I almost have to tie my hands down to keep them off my phone but I manage to not call Jesse. My patience is thin by the time we meet up on the way to humanities the next day. "Someone was grinning like a hyena yesterday."

He stops and we stand at the entrance to the freshmen building. A huge smile spreads. "The coach from UT is coming to watch me play next week. This is huge, princess. It's everything I need because it isn't far from Harley and Ozzy and UT has an awesome law school."

I throw my arms around his neck. "That is awesome. I'm so happy for you."

He picks me up and we spin for a few seconds before he puts me down on the ground. He looks at my face and I can't force myself to let go of him. "I'm going to UT too."

I'm puzzled by his expression. I don't know what it means.

199

"You never told me that."

I remain inside the friend-zone boundaries and bite my tongue instead of telling him how this solves our problems. I don't point out the obvious—that both of us at UT will make it possible for us to be together. "It's my mom's alma mater. Ryan and Maggie went there too."

I realize I'm still holding on to him. "Sorry." I release my hold and bend over to pick up my backpack from the sidewalk. "I'm really excited for you."

We enter the building and he bumps my shoulder like we're old chums. "It's okay. Friends can hug. I'm pretty sure they do it every day."

I halfheartedly smile at his dismissal of our embrace. We both know it's based on more than friendship, even if neither of us acknowledges it.

I SPEND the rest of the week struggling with my every move around Jesse. Fighting what comes naturally is exhausting. Averting my instinct to touch his skin and tell him how much I love him grows increasingly difficult with each passing day. I question if he's feeling the same.

We sit at our secluded table at the back of the library, a place I've grown to love. Jesse catches my attention several times when he looks up from his work. I think he's about to say something each time but then he looks away, as if he's changed his mind.

After the fifth time, I drop my pencil and wait until he does it again. "What?"

He shrugs. "I didn't say anything."

We both reach to catch my pencil as it threatens to roll onto the floor but he's faster. "You've looked at me a half-dozen times like you want to. Spit it out already."

He shrugs again. It makes me crazy when he does that. "It's nothing."

It's been days since I've had any skin-on-skin contact with him and I can't stand it any longer. I reach out to touch his hand. "Tell me. I want to know what's so fluster-worthy."

He grins. "I'm going to see my little brothers on Sunday."

I feel utter joy in my heart for him. "Aww … that's great. I know you're excited. It's been a while. I'll bet they're super happy about that." He seems restless. "Is something wrong with the boys?"

He shakes his head. "No, nothing like that. I was just thinking of … maybe asking you to go with me."

I don't answer because I'm pondering what this means. This isn't a simple invite to the movies. It's huge. He's asking me to meet his brothers, the two little people who mean the world to him.

"I completely understand if you don't want to, so don't feel like you have to say yes."

"Yes. I want to go." My heart inflates almost to the point of bursting. I fight the tears because I'm afraid he'll withdraw his invitation if I make too much of it. I turn away and look up at the ceiling, willing my eyes to suck the moisture back in. "I love kids. Sounds like fun. What time?"

"My visitation begins at one. Can you meet me around twelve thirty at the garage?"

I can't be more blissed out but I keep my elation in check because I don't want to ruin this. "Sure."

We finish our assignment early and he tells me about Harley and Ozzy and how he's parented them since his mom was always MIA or drugged out. He tells me comical things about their lives to keep the mood light but the reality of the situation is just plain pitiful. I laugh about his adventures in parenting, but I'm furious with a dead woman. The things he's been forced to endure are unfair at best, but it's clear how much he loves Harley and Ozzy. He wouldn't take anything in the world in exchange for those two little boys.

It's Sunday and I'm out the door to meet Jesse at Earl's garage. I'm on time for once, but he's still there before me.

He gets out of his truck and walks over to my driver's side window. He leans inside and my heart almost stops. Gah, I want to lick him. "Do you mind if we take your car?" he says. "It's probably best if we don't leave an unattended convertible with an expensive sound system in Collinsville."

"No problem."

He locks his truck and gets into my car. I inhale deeply because he smells so damn good. "Their reaction to you should be interesting. I've never brought a girl with me."

I'd be disappointed if he had. "Should I be scared?"

"No, they'll be fine once they see how you are."

This could be a loaded question. "How am I?"

I wait for the answer but he says nothing. Just when I've decided he isn't going to answer, he says, "Wonderful … that's how you are." His voice is so soft, it's nearly a whisper.

I wish I could kiss him.

"Will we be allowed to take the boys somewhere?"

"I hope so. Brian and Heather are a nice couple but interacting with Harley and Ozzy in their home is uncomfortable."

That's understandable. "Have they allowed you to take them out before?"

"I had them for a few hours on their birthday."

I'm confused. "They're twins?"

"No, but they might as well be. They have the same birthday, one year apart."

That must have been like taking care of twins. "That's neat. How long ago was that?"

"It was the day after I spent the night with you."

"Oh." No matter how I try to keep the conversation safe, it always ends up reminding me of how we once were—and how desperately I want to be there again.

I pull into the drive and see two little heads bobbing up and down in a big window at the front of the house. I laugh at the sight. "I think I just spotted two little boys eager to see their big brother."

Jesse opens the door. "I'm eager to see them too. It's been too long."

The front door swings open and two of the cutest little boys ever run across the lawn, tackling Jesse in the grass. He picks them up and swings them around at the same time. "Oh, I missed you guys so much!"

They're adorable. And they have Jesse's eyes.

"We missed you too, Jess," the bigger one says.

Jesse puts them down and the smaller one chimes in. "You said you'd come back and you did."

He puts his finger on the little one's nose and presses. "I always keep my promises, you knucklehead. You know that."

"We know," they say together.

"I have someone I want you to meet." I walk over to the boys and crouch so I'm on their level. "This is Claire."

I hold out my hand and the bigger boy takes it. "You must be Harley. I've heard some very good things about you."

"Are you Jesse's girlfriend?" he asks.

Jesse saves me by answering his brother for me. "Claire is my friend and I wanted her to come meet you and Ozzy because she's very special to me."

Harley giggles. "That means she's your girlfriend."

Jesse looks at me and shrugs.

Ozzy's hiding behind Jesse's leg peeking around to see me. Jesse told me he tends to be shy around new people so I squat lower to make him more comfortable. "Hello, Ozzy. It's very nice to meet you."

He sails from behind Jesse's leg and launches himself at me, giving a hug I wasn't expecting—but one I welcome. I put my arms around this sweet boy and smile at Jesse when I see the astonishment on his face. Ozzy puts his arms up and I lift him to sit on my hip like an oversized toddler. He places his head on my shoulder and I let him because it seems to make him happy. And me too.

"He never does that with anyone. I'm not sure he's even hugged Mrs. Stevens that way and he's been living with her for months."

"I guess he's like his older brother. He has great taste in girls." I laugh.

WE TALK with Heather and Brian for a little while and then secure the boys into my car. Jesse decides on the park since it's what they always do and he likes them to have a routine with him.

I occasionally look into my rearview mirror at the boys sitting so tall in their booster seats. I've never driven children in my car so it feels a little strange.

"Claire, you can at least do the speed limit," Jesse says.

I look at the speedometer and realize I'm driving super slow. "Sorry."

I look at what beautiful little boys Harley and Ozzy are and I can't understand how a mother and grandmother could care so little about them. I hate them.

I reach over and touch Jesse's hand. "I packed a picnic lunch in case we got to take them out. It's in the trunk. Just sandwiches and chips since I didn't know what they liked. Nothing special."

I look forward as I drive but I can see him staring at me and I don't know why. "Is that not okay?"

He reaches for my hand and brings it to his lips like old times. He kisses the top and grazes it along his face. "I know it's not part of the friend pact but I have to tell you something. I love you more right now than I ever have. No one has ever done anything like that for them."

I hear Harley's voice in the backseat. "I told you she was his girlfriend."

Wow. I never dreamed peanut butter and jelly sandwiches would make him declare his love. It's shocking how much a simple act means to him, and that gives me a glimpse into how terrible his childhood must've been.

We sit on a blanket under a large tree and I divvy out food. "Jesse brought us a birthday cake and we ate it at the picnic tables, but we've never had a real picnic on the ground before," Harley says, biting into his sandwich. His mouth is full and he keeps on talking. "I like this a lot."

"Don't talk while you have food in your mouth," Jesse tells him.

Ozzy isn't eating and looks deep in thought. "Are you not hungry?"

"I am but I was thinking about something."

I'm curious about what a four-year-old can think so hard about. "What's on your mind?"

"Do you and Jesse kiss?"

His question catches me off guard and I don't know how to answer a young child with a question like that. I look at Jesse but he's laughing too hysterically to be of any help. "We've kissed."

"Do you love each other?" Oh God. I look to Jesse again for help but he puts his hands up, letting me know I have this one all on my own.

If he isn't going to help me, then he doesn't get to be privy to my answer. I lean over and whisper in Ozzy's ear. "I love Jesse very much."

Ozzy pulls me down to his level so he can whisper in my ear. "Will you marry Jesse and be my momma so we can be a family again?"

The blood drains from my face and Jesse interrupts our whisper session by telling Ozzy to stop stalling and eat. I look at him with gratitude because I have no idea how I was going to respond to that.

We finish eating and spend our time at the playground. They groan when Jesse announces it's time to go back, but they obey without a fuss.

It's heartbreaking to watch Jesse leave them but I know it's in their best interests for the moment. He promises them he'll be back soon, so it makes the goodbye a little easier.

We get into my car and I see their little heads bobbing in the window as we drive away. "That was fun."

"What did Ozzy whisper in your ear?"

I hesitate because I'm not sure I want to tell him. I ponder leaving it a secret for just me and Ozzy but decide to let Jesse in on it. "He asked me to marry you so I could be his momma and we could be a family."

He looks choked up. "I'm sorry about that." His voice cracks.

"Don't be. I'm not. It was very sweet of him to think of me that way."

"They adore you. I knew they would. Especially Ozzy."

"They're great. Thanks for inviting me."

"You needed to see what my life is going to be like when I get them back. It's not going to be frat parties and getting drunk with friends. My world will be about getting through school as fast as possible while I take care of two little kids."

Omigod. The reason behind the invite suddenly registers with me. He wants me to see the responsibility he has to those two little boys. He's trying to use them to scare me away. "You didn't bring me here to hang out and have fun. This is about you freaking out because we're going to the same college. You don't want me to get my hopes up about getting back together once we're at UT." He doesn't deny my accusation and it's because I'm right. "Do you really think your responsibility to those boys will send me running?"

"I thought it would," he admits.

"Do you think so little of me?"

"I wouldn't fault you for running. There are times I think about it myself but I love them too much. They're a huge responsibility— not one every teenager wants to be tied to, so I want you to see what's on my plate sooner rather than later."

"You were right to show me but you're wrong about the other part. You're not going to scare me off that easily."

CHAPTER THIRTY-FIVE

JESSE BOONE

SEEING CLAIRE WITH MY BROTHERS CONFIRMS HOW RIGHT SHE IS FOR ME AND how wrong I am for her.

Did I make the wrong decision by taking Claire to meet Harley and Ozzy? They're crazy about her, especially Ozzy, and she fell in love with them as well.

Have I opened a door I can't close by allowing her into that part of my life?

I pull into the drive and see Rita's car. Shit! I really want to avoid her today. It's getting time for her to send me out again.

Inside, she's sitting on the couch smoking. Always smoking. It's something I've come to absolutely despise since I quit. "'Bout time you brought your ass back."

"I went to see Harley and Ozzy."

"I've got some dime bags on the table." I'm not surprised when she doesn't ask about the boys.

She takes a long drag and blows upward. I thought being around the smoke after I quit would make me want to do it again, but it's had the opposite effect. I hate it.

I look over the table and see a dozen bags of marijuana. "I can't sell all of that tonight."

"You can or you won't sleep here tonight." I'm so sick of her threats.

I need to study for my calculus test instead of going out to be a thug for her, but that's the beauty of having Rita as a grandmother. She doesn't care and that's going to make leaving here and never coming back so damn easy.

I yank the bags of dope off the table and go back to my truck. I head south on the road to Collinsville because I won't infiltrate East Franklin with her trash.

I make some calls on my way to line up sales. They're the same customers I've sold to for years and luckily I'll have half the stash sold at one stop.

At the apartment complex I've frequented a thousand times, I get out and knock on the same door I always go to first. It swings open and a big, burly guy stands in the doorway. He puts his fist out for a bump. "Jess, my man. Good to see you. You haven't been around in a while."

I don't want to be here now, either, but I am because I don't have a choice. "Yeah, I don't make it over here a lot since I moved."

"Come in, dude. Have a seat."

I don't want to get stuck talking, or worse, staying while they sample the merchandise. "Nah, I can't stay. I've got more deliveries to make." I say it like the whole thing is cool with me.

"Come in while I get your money. We can't make this exchange standing in the door for anybody to see." He goes inside and walks toward the back of the apartment.

Shit. I don't want to do this but he's right. I follow him inside and close the door. Several guys are hanging out in the living room. I give them a nod.

"Hey, you're that little shit who ripped me off a few months ago," one of them says as he comes up off the couch.

I don't remember him but he's probably telling the truth. Twyla had me shorting people left and right.

He's fast and I don't have time to react. He punches me in the face and my blood sprays the wall. One of the guys yells, "Beat his ass, Matt!"

He wrestles me to the floor and I get on top, punching him a few good times, but his friends aren't going to sit back and watch.

Another one comes off the couch. "We'll teach you to come around after ripping somebody off."

An excruciating pain follows the hard kick to my back. I take a second kick to my abdomen and then a strike to the back of my head. A warm ooze follows, flowing onto my neck and shoulders.

I propel myself toward the door and swing it open because there's no way I can win this uneven fight. I speed out of the apartment complex and onto the road toward Rita's.

I reach into my pocket and discover I lost every last bag of dope in the shuffle. I slam my fist against the steering wheel of my truck. I knew better than to go in with all of it. Rookie mistake.

I dread the fight I'm about to have with Rita. I wonder if she'll throw me out.

I go into the trailer but she only glances in my direction. "That was fast. You could be getting as good as your mother was." She brings her Camel to her lips but doesn't take a drag because she begins having a coughing episode. She's been doing that a lot lately —I strongly suspect she has lung cancer.

When she finishes coughing, she looks at me. "Did you charge those Franklin kids extra like I told you?"

I'm standing in front of her covered in blood. Can she not see I've had the hell beat out of me—that I could've been killed? Does she not care at all?

I remember who I'm talking about and register how little she'd care if someone killed me, as long as she got her money. "I got jumped by three guys and they got all the pot."

I don't have to wait long for a response. "Then you owe me a hundred and twenty bucks. Better go get into that stash you're hiding and pay up."

I go into my room and pull out the money I've been saving—it's every dollar I have—and return to the living room where she's sitting. I throw my entire savings on the coffee table in front of her and walk back to my room.

"I bet you won't be so stupid next time, boy."

I get into the shower to wash away the blood. When I wash my hair, it burns like hell. I'm going to need stitches. I wince just thinking about how sore I'll be in the morning.

I use a mirror to look at the back of my head and see a continuous bleed that doesn't stop with applied pressure. Damn. I have to go to the hospital.

It's almost midnight by the time I'm released from the ER. I return to Rita's, do my homework, and lie down to get a little sleep before I have to be up for school.

As I suspect, I'm sore as hell when I wake up a few short hours later. I stir in my bed for a minute, dreading the actual movement of getting up. I go into the kitchen and take a couple of over-the-counter pain relievers and then stand under the hottest shower Rita's water heater will produce.

I examine my swollen, bruised face. Claire is going to have a fit but that's not the worst part. She'll want an explanation for how it happened. I consider lying to her, but what's the good in that?

Maybe she'll finally get the picture and realize I'm no good for her.

I inspect the stitches and man, it looks awful because the doctor shaved a big patch on the back of my head. It would look better to buzz my whole head but I don't have clippers. I wish I could cover it with a cap but the school doesn't allow them. There's absolutely no hiding this from my princess.

She's going to go apeshit.

CLAIRE SPIES me as I'm walking to calculus and her smile fades as she stands at her locker, Forbes and Payton by her side. Her eyes never leave me once she notices my bruised face and I'm certain she sees the gash and bald spot on the back of my head when I walk past.

I dread second period.

Payton's eyes are huge when she comes into calculus. She sits in front of me, as she's become accustomed to doing. I already know I'll never be lucky enough for her to keep her restless lips quiet. "You look like shit."

"Thanks, but I wish you'd tell me how you really feel."

"What happened, besides getting the hell beat out of you?" she asks.

I shake my head, letting her know I'm not going there with her.

"Claire, is going crazy but you already know that, right?"

Yep.

"You want me to put a little makeup on that pretty face for you, Kemosabe?" she laughs.

"I'm good."

It's time to face Claire before I'd like. She watches every step I take from the time I enter the classroom until I'm seated next to her.

Her face is pale. "What happened to you?" she whispers.

"Rita told me I had to go out and sell when I got home last night. I got my ass kicked by three dopeheads and stayed in the emergency room until almost midnight getting the back of my head stitched up."

"Turn around," she orders.

I do as she tells me and she gasps in horror. "You can't stay there anymore."

I laugh. "Where am I going to go? I have no one. I'm lucky Rita lets me stay with her."

"You're there so you can make money for her. Don't mistake that for luck."

"I have nowhere to go and she took all my money to make up for the dope I lost while I was getting the hell beat out of me."

"Your mother almost got you killed and Rita is going to finish the job if we don't get you out of there." She places her tiny hand on top of my much larger one. "I don't know where you'll go but we'll think of something."

CHAPTER THIRTY-SIX

CLAIRE DEVERAUX

No way I'm letting Jesse's grandmother get him killed.

I spend the rest of the day racking my brain, thinking of a way to get him away from Rita. Everything I think of requires monetary resources he doesn't have and because I'm at a total loss for what to do, I resort to the only choice I have—my parents.

I find my mom in the kitchen preparing dinner. I don't get a word out before I start crying. "What's wrong, Claire?"

"It's Jesse."

"Did something happen?" She steps away from the stove, placing her oven mitts on the counter.

"His grandmother sent him out last night and three guys beat him to a pulp."

"I knew this was coming."

"He has nowhere to go but he can't live with her anymore. She's going to get him killed." She looks at me, saying nothing. "The back of his head has a huge gash in it and his face looks horrible. I don't even want to see what his body looks like beneath his clothes because every time he moved, he looked like he was in agony."

She sighs. "What do you expect me to do?"

"You are his counselor. That must place some kind of responsibility on you to help him."

"He's aged out. I can't call child welfare to pick him up."

"Humanity. That's all I'm asking for. One human aiding another who can't help himself. This isn't his choice. He's being forced to do this for survival."

She stands with her hands on her hips. "I can't do anything without talking to your father first."

I throw my arms around her, squeezing her tightly. "When will Dad be home?"

"He told me he'd be here for dinner so maybe within the hour, but you know how an hour can turn into two or three with your dad."

I spend the next two hours pacing the floor waiting on my dad to come home from work. I propel myself, wrapping my arms around him when he finally walks through the door. "Well, what in the world have I done to deserve this?" I can't help it. I'm already crying. "What is it, baby?"

My mom calls out from the kitchen. "Claire, let your dad get in the door. We'll discuss everything over dinner."

I back off and allow my dad into the house, although I'm dying to tell him everything. I help my mom prepare our plates and we sit at the dining room table. "I'm a little nervous about what's going on," he says.

My mom starts. "There's been an incident with Jesse but I'm going to let her tell you."

I start at the beginning and tell my dad everything I know about Jesse since my mother is still bound by oath to not discuss him or his case. My dad stops eating and listens as I describe a very sad story about Twyla's three precious boys. I sum up the tale by sharing Jesse's current situation and how he'll certainly be dead before graduation if we don't do something to help him escape his grandmother.

My dad is shocked by the details of Jesse's horrific life. "Your mother and I have to talk about this without you. Go upstairs and we'll call you down after we've made a decision."

Alone in my room, five minutes turns into twenty and twenty turns into forty-five. At sixty, I'm standing in the middle of my bedroom ready to have a full-blown panic attack but then my mom comes to my door. "You can come down now."

I feel close to passing out. Once I establish that I'm okay, I follow my mom to the living room and sit across from my parents.

I hear the thudding of my heart in my ears and it's close to drowning the sound of my dad's voice. "This is a hard one for us. Jesse's life has been horrific but we see so much potential in him. He's very intelligent and a highly gifted athlete. There's no doubt he'll go on to do great things if he's given half an opportunity." My heart soars.

"But here comes the hard part." My heart sputters.

"We agree that Jesse needs to leave his grandmother's home as soon as possible. The debate is what do we do with him once we get him out," my dad says.

I don't know. I haven't thought that far ahead.

"We could help him get into an apartment but that doesn't seem like the right answer since we have concerns about the depth of your feelings for him. We think putting him in a place with no adult guidance could set you up for a situation you aren't ready to handle. You're not adults so you're not ready to make adult decisions about having sex, and we know that's where it will lead if you're given the freedom."

I turn every shade of red as my dad talks about Jesse and I making the decision to have sex. He would kill me and Jesse both if he knew we'd already gone there and done that.

"We've debated back and forth but we've decided Jesse can live here on a temporary basis until we're able to make more permanent arrangements."

I realize I've been holding my breath for far too long when I gasp.

"We can control the privacy between you if we're here to supervise, but there will be conditions. There will be no hanky-panky in this house. Under no circumstance will we tolerate that. This is about helping Jesse get safe, not about moving him in here so you can play footsie under the table. If we find out there's been any inappropriate contact between the two of you, he will have to leave immediately."

I get up and run to my dad first and throw my arms around him. "I understand."

"Thank you, Mom. I will never forget this as long as I live." This is a huge concession for her to let go of everything she knows about Jesse. It can't be easy.

"I want to go get him now."

My dad is humored by my urgency but he doesn't understand the dire straits of Jesse's situation. "It's almost nine o'clock. We need to talk to him about this first. We can't show up on his doorstep and tell him to pack his stuff because we're there to rescue him."

"Yes, we can. I promise you he'll happily leave any way he can because he wants out of there so badly."

I can't stand the thought of him staying there another night.

I start to cry because I have an overwhelming urgency to get Jesse out of that place tonight. "Please, Dad. What if something happens to him before the morning? You didn't see how bad he was beaten last night. It took more than fifty stitches to put his head back together. You know more than all of us how bad it had to be if it required that many stitches."

He looks like he's thinking it over so I strike again. "I won't sleep tonight if he's still in that place."

My mom nods, giving her approval, and my dad gives in as well. "Get the Batmobile, Robin."

I'm flooded with relief. "Thank you. Thank you so much."

I grab my phone while Dad gets his keys. I try to call Jesse several times as we drive to his house but I get no answer. "He's not answering. I hope that isn't a bad sign."

My dad doesn't say anything and I pick at my freshly manicured nails. He reaches over and grabs my hand to stop my nervous fidgeting. "It's going to okay."

I won't relax until I see Jesse safely out of that drug house.

We pull up and Jesse's truck is in the yard so I relax a little, knowing we've at least found him. I look at Dad before we get out —I can't begin to tell him how grateful I am and what this kind of help for Jesse means to me. It's more than I could ever hope for. "Thank you again."

He squeezes my hand. "Come on, let's go save this boy you love."

We get out of the car and go up the steps to the trailer's front door. We stand there waiting and I begin to feel something isn't right. I knock again. "Jesse, it's Claire."

He doesn't come to the door. Doom creeps up on me. Something is definitely off about this. "This isn't right, Dad. He didn't answer his phone and now he's not coming to the door."

I walk over to the window and try to look in but I'm too short to see over the piece of furniture pushed up against the window. "I can't see anything."

I reach for the doorknob, but my dad stops me.

"You can't open the door and go in there. There could be a … reason he isn't coming to the door." He's suggesting Jesse may be with another girl, but I know better.

"He's not with another girl, Dad." I laugh. "But if he is, I need you to help me bury his body."

He stretches on tiptoes to peer in the window and his eyes grow large. He runs to the front door and tries to turn the doorknob, but it's locked. "What is it, Dad? What do you see?"

"Stand back, Claire." He pushes me away from the door and kicks it.

"What are you doing?"

He doesn't reply as he kicks the flimsy aluminum door again, sending it flying open. He runs inside and I follow behind, uncertain of what I'll find.

Jesse is pale, almost gray, and lying on the floor in a pool of blood. My dad leans over him, listening for his breath and feeling for a pulse. "Call 911. Now."

I reach for my phone and dial with shaky fingers. My father attempts to resuscitate the boy I love. Nothing is happening. He isn't waking up. He isn't moving at all.

We're too late. He's already dead.

My mind immediately goes into denial. He can't be gone because everything was on its way to working out for us.

It feels like an eternity passes as we wait for the ambulance to arrive. My dad moves out of their way and collapses from doing CPR so long.

The emergency crew applies sticky pads to Jesse's chest to assess his cardiac activity and I lose my breath when I hear them say he has none. He's in full cardiac arrest.

The harder I try to breathe, the less air I'm able to get. I hear my dad telling me to slow my breathing but I can't and my body only tolerates it for a minute before it gives way and I collapse to the floor.

Everything goes black. The boy I love is dead.

CHAPTER THIRTY-SEVEN

JESSE BOONE

I WAKE IN THE HOSPITAL AND TURN MY HEAD TO SEE WHO'S SITTING IN THE chair at my bedside, slumped forward asleep on my bed. My eyes are severely out of focus and I can't see the face but I recognize the long auburn hair splayed across the bedspread.

It's my princess.

I look at my hand and see she's gripping it tightly, even in her sleep.

My mind is foggy but not enough to forget how this is so similar to the other time she sat at my bedside in the hospital. I suspect this time is going to be different.

I'm connected to lots of monitors. I can't be positive I'm not seeing double because there's too many to count. The one concerning me most is the tube in my mouth—connected to a ventilator. I know what it is because this isn't the first time to have one doing my breathing for me.

This is not good.

I'm still confused but I know one thing. The tube in my mouth and throat has to come out before I seriously lose my shit.

I squeeze Claire's hand and she slowly lifts her head from my

218

bed. She smiles when she sees my eyes and lifts her hand to touch my face. "Hey, you," she cries.

I want to respond with my usual "Hey, princess," but I can't. I point to the tube in my mouth.

She shoots up from her chair and hits the call light. "I'm supposed to tell the nurses if you wake up enough to fight the breathing tube so they can take it out."

I stare at the ceiling praying I don't completely lose it before a nurse gets in here to get this damn thing out of me. Just when I think I might go apeshit, one appears. "Glad to see you're back with us, Mr. Boone."

The nurse screws a syringe into the tube and pulls back. "My name is Angie and I'm going to take this out on the count of three. One. Two. Three." She pulls the tube and I gasp and sputter like a newborn baby.

"Your throat is going to be sore because you've been intubated for a week. You're lucky. If you hadn't woken up today, you were going down for a trach tomorrow, young man."

"How long have I been here?" My voice is weak and squeaky.

"Seven very long days," Claire says.

"Since your condition has changed, I need to do a quick assessment so I can call the doctor."

She turns to Claire. "I need you to step out for a minute. I'll let you back in as soon as I finish." Claire doesn't budge. "I promise I'll let you back in as soon as I can."

Princess leans over and kisses my forehead. "I'll just be right outside that door. I'm not going anywhere. Got it?"

"Got it," I squeak. I'm a little embarrassed by how feminine I sound.

Angie does her thing and keeps her promise to Claire. She returns to my side and takes my hand in hers. "How do you feel?"

"Like hell."

Tears spill from her eyes. "I had to listen to the paramedics talk back and forth about how you didn't have a heartbeat. They had to shock you. Do you know what that means? You were clinically dead."

I'm still incredibly weak but I need her near me. "Come here," I whisper.

She's sitting on the edge of my bed and crawls up next to me. "The nurses won't like this. They'll make me get up."

I lean my head over until it touches hers. "Then we'll stay like this until one of them makes you get up."

I don't have much voice in me but we don't need to talk. Just being next to one another is enough for the moment.

Angie returns but doesn't tell Claire to get out of my bed. "Do you want a pillow, Claire?"

"I'm good, thank you."

We're silent and motionless for about a half hour. "The police will be here soon. They wanted to be notified as soon as you woke up. They need to take your statement about what happened, and they told us to not talk about it with you because you could become confused."

I'll never tell her anything about what happened.

There's a knock on the door and a man in a fancy suit comes into my room. "Hello, Claire."

"Hi, Uncle Bill. Thank you for coming." She gives him a big hug. "This is my dad's brother, Bill. He's an attorney and he's going to be with you when the police question you about what happened."

Why would I need an attorney? "Am I in trouble for something?" I ask.

"Not at the moment, but Warren and Deandra think you should be represented and from what they've told me, I agree. This could get out of hand very quickly."

She squeezes my hand. "Everything is going to be okay. My parents asked Uncle Bill to come because they want to help you."

"I don't understand. Why would they do that?"

She's still holding my hand tightly. "Because I asked them to. And because they believe you have potential if given half a chance. You should give yourself more credit. You're not so bad, you know?"

"I need to speak with Jesse before the police get here," Bill says.

She leans over and kisses my forehead. "I'll come back after you're finished."

I don't want her to go but I know she can't stay.

Bill opens his briefcase. "We don't have much time. Tell me everything that happened that night."

I give him the quick version before the police arrive and his only advice is to tell the truth.

There's a knock on the door and two men come into my room. "Mr. Boone, my name is Detective Buchanan and this is my partner, Detective Kline."

The detectives take out notepads and one of them places a recorder on the table in front of me. "Mr. Boone, tell us in your own words what happened the night of October twentieth."

Despite being unconscious for a week, I remember everything as though it just happened. "I came home to my grandmother's house a little before nine o'clock. There was no sign of forced entry and the door was locked, so I unlocked it and walked into the living room. The place looked like a tornado had been through it. The furniture was turned upside down. The couch cushions were sliced open and stuffing was thrown everywhere. A man ran toward me from the hallway and we struggled in the living room for a minute or so. I was overpowering him, but then I felt a sharp pain in my lower back and I went down."

"Mr. Boone, did you recognize either of the men?"

Chills come over me. "The one who stabbed me in the back—it was Wayne Moore."

"You said that you felt a sharp pain and then you went down. How did you recognize the man if he stabbed you from behind?"

"I spent the better part of my childhood being kicked by him. He always told me the same thing when I was a little kid on the floor. 'You better stay down, boy.' That's what he said to me that night. There's no mistaking him."

"Why were these men in your house? What were they looking for?" Detective Kline asks.

I seriously consider my answer. If I tell the truth, I'm out on my keister. I won't have a roof over my head. If I lie to protect my grandmother so I can go back to that house, I'll end up dead before my nineteenth birthday. Either way, I won't have a place to stay. "Drugs."

They both scribble on their notepads. "Your drugs?" Detective Kline questions.

"They were there to steal my grandmother's."

"Your grandmother is a drug dealer?" Detective Buchanan laughs.

He probably pictures a gray-haired lady sitting in her recliner knitting. "Have you met my grandmother? She's not a kind, nurturing woman. Meet her once and you'll know I'm telling the truth."

"Mr. Boone, I'm quite familiar with your grandmother, as are most people at the station so I know you're telling the truth. I asked to see if you'd lie or not."

They gather their things. "Dr. and Mrs. Deveraux seem to think a lot of you and have done a great job of convincing us to stop looking at you for wrongdoing. I advise you to take them up on this opportunity they're offering," Detective Buchanan says. "You won't get another like it."

What is he talking about? I look at Bill, but he gives nothing away.

"Thank you for your cooperation, Mr. Boone. And just so you know, Wayne Moore was killed last night in a motor vehicle accident while driving under the influence—probably high on whatever he stole the night he almost killed you. It's a simple case of what goes around comes around, if you ask me."

"Detectives, if you're finished here, then I believe I am as well." My Deveraux-appointed attorney gathers his papers as the detectives leave my room. "I think that went well. I don't think you should expect any type of charges to be brought against you."

I'm damn lucky and I know it. I breezed through that by the skin of my teeth. "Thank you for coming and for your counsel."

He closes his briefcase. "Not a problem. But I don't expect to get another call from my brother about getting you out of legal trouble. This is your only chance with him. He won't be so generous a second time when it comes to his daughter."

"What did the detective mean when he spoke about the opportunity the Deverauxs are giving me?" I ask.

"That's for them to discuss with you."

Claire appears in the door. "I saw the detectives leave. Is it okay for me to come back now?"

"We're done. I was just about to leave," Bill says.

Claire enters and gives her uncle another hug. "No worries, Claire Bear. It's going to be fine."

She walks her uncle out and I'm impatient for her to return. I'm dying to know what kind of opportunity everyone is talking about.

Princess returns to my room and I want to ask her immediately. However, I don't because I'm not exactly sure what to ask. She climbs back into my bed and nuzzles into me. We're quiet but my mind races with possibilities.

"I need to talk to you about something," she says.

"Okay."

"The evening you were attacked, my father and I were there to find you. The plan was to help you get away from Rita but then all of this happened. I don't think we have to worry about you going back there."

"I won't be going back there no matter what, so be on the lookout for a nice cardboard box. It doesn't have to be fancy."

"Stop." She laughs. "My parents want you to live with us until they can work out a more permanent arrangement."

So, this is the opportunity the detective spoke about? I'm astonished. And speechless.

"What do you think?" she asks.

"I think I love you. I think you have truly wonderful parents for giving me a chance."

"Jesse, I love you with all of my being and this is only the beginning of the rest of our lives together."

I laugh. "This isn't a great beginning, princess. I hope it's not a baseline of things to come."

She touches my face. "Don't worry. There are wonderful things in store for us. And as soon as you're better, I'm going to show you exactly what they are."

EPILOGUE

CLAIRE DEVERAUX

As usual, I'm running late. I look at my watch and see I'm supposed to be at my parents' house in thirty minutes for the birthday party, but I'm standing in the sporting goods store trying to choose gifts.

I take out my phone and choose the contact at the top of my favorites list. "Hey, I'm running late as usual and I need help picking gifts. Any ideas?"

After hearing several suggestions, I finally make my decision. I quickly check out and drive to the party. Only ten minutes late this time.

I walk through the door with gifts in hand and my dad rushes over to help me. "You really shouldn't be carrying all of this at the same time. You know your balance is already off-center. You could fall."

"Sorry. I'll try to remember that."

He takes the gifts and carries them to the bar where the others are. Two little angels without wings run toward me, both throwing their arms around my expanding abdomen.

"Claire, I want to feel the baby kick. Make him move for me," says the little face pressed against my belly.

These boys are so determined. "You keep saying him, but what if it's a her?"

"Oh, it's a him. There's no doubt in my mind." Harley is so confident.

"Let's try this. I'll eat a big piece of birthday cake. I guarantee he or she will be moving like crazy after that. Will that work?"

I watch the beautiful boy's pale blue eyes light up as he agrees with my plan. "Come on. I think Mom is ready for us to cut the cake."

We go into the kitchen and I see a chocolate cake with seven candles on one side and eight on the other. To them, there is no other way.

My parents adopted Harley and Ozzy right before they turned six and seven. My mother offered them separate cakes when their birthday rolled around, but they found out real quick that Jesse's way is the only way for these precious boys. I love that they want to stick to tradition and I feel obligated to help keep Jesse's traditions alive in them.

My mom's working on finding a lighter for the candles when I feel warm, muscular arms wrap around me from behind. "How my baby momma doing?" Jesse whispers in my ear.

I laugh hysterically. I love when he says that. "Yo' baby momma doing good."

"No pains today?" he asks.

"I didn't say that." I'm pregnant. I have pain all day, every day.

"Think you can pull off giving birth to our son or daughter on our brothers' birthday?"

I think about how that sounds. "Jesse, someone who didn't know us would think that sounds really messed up."

He puts his hands on my great pregnant abdomen and leans down to talk to my belly. "Little baby Boone ... it would be really cool if you could pull off being born on your Uncle Harley and Uncle Ozzy's birthday."

"Trying to coax this baby out into the world today has nothing to do with how anxious you are to find out if it's a boy or girl, right?"

This man has nearly driven me crazy since our ultrasound. He had immediate not-finding-out regret.

"It has absolutely everything to do with it. I'm going crazy here, woman," he says.

"It was your idea to not find out what we're having so suck it up, buddy. I have another week until my due date. This baby will come when he or she is ready and not a minute before."

I laugh at his childish anxiousness because he's worse than Harley and Ozzy put together.

My mom laughs at our conversation as she lights the candles on the cake. "Jesse, I hope this baby takes after you because if it takes after Claire, it won't come until next year."

I roll my eyes. "Whatever."

We sing "Happy Birthday" to the boys and I'm more than happy to have a big piece of birthday cake to entice the baby into moving. I add a big scoop of ice cream for good measure and drink a cola while Jesse watches me. He thinks I should always have water. "I know what you're thinking and Dad says I can have one a day."

Jesse puts his hands up. "I didn't say a word, princess."

"You were thinking it because I saw it on your face." I don't have time to dwell on it because I feel a big kick. "Ozzy, come here, quick. The baby is moving just for you."

He runs over and puts his head and hands against my belly. I feel a big movement and I wait to hear Ozzy's response. "He kicked my ear."

Ozzy looks up at Jesse. "He's going to be a kicker like me, not a quarterback."

Jesse puts his hand on top of Ozzy's head and musses his hair. "You better watch it, little knucklehead."

I laugh and feel a pop, a prelude to the warm water flowing down my legs. My heart races a little as I realize what's happening.

Jesse notices the reaction on my face as I look down. "What's wrong?"

I point to my legs. "Looks like this baby is going to take after you."

"What do you mean?" he asks.

"The baby isn't going to be late like me."

Jesse pales a little. "He's coming now?"

"My water just broke."

THE DUST SETTLES from the delivery and the rush of family coming in and out to see our little miracle. It's finally just the three of us.

Jesse stares at me as I hold our baby on my chest. He smiles, though he's been super quiet since we arrived at the hospital.

"What are you thinking?"

He doesn't look away from our daughter. "That I have two princesses now."

"Were you hoping for a boy?"

He reaches up to stroke her head. "No. I sort of feel like I've already raised boys so I wanted a girl. Now that I've seen her, I can't imagine life without her."

She sighs one of those cute little sounds only a newborn can make. "Me, either. She's perfect."

I think of all the changes we've experienced the past few years and I still can't believe the way things have happened for us.

I thought it was the end the night Wayne Moore and his accomplice came into Jesse's house and attacked him, but that night was our beginning. Believing the one you love is gone forever does something to you that words can't explain.

Once Jesse recovered from his second near-death experience, he came to live with us and my parents fell in love with him as much as I had, especially when they saw I refused any future that didn't include him. He didn't get his football scholarship because he was unable to finish out the season, but it didn't matter. He bumped me from valedictorian and got a full academic scholarship to UT. My parents took in the boys and later adopted them so we could go to college without the stress of raising them. It worked out well—my mother suffered from a case of empty nest syndrome after Jesse and I were away at university.

Against the advice of my parents, we married before finishing college because that crazy, intense love we have for each other didn't lessen. A few months later, this little surprise slipped in on us.

I touch his hand to get his attention. "I know she wasn't planned, but thank you for giving her to me."

"I still need to figure out how I gave you that one so I don't turn around and give you another before I mean to."

I think I know the culprit. "I'm pretty sure it has something to do with that see-through nighty I wore on your birthday and a playful pole dance on the bedpost, if you'll think back for a minute."

He scrunches his forehead in concentration and a smile spreads. "You think that was when she happened?"

"I'm positive."

He looks back at her. "She's the best birthday present I've ever been given. Thank you."

I stroke her soft back. "Did we decide on Finley?"

"Finley Elizabeth Boone." He says it out loud, like he's test-driving it. "Yeah, I love it."

He leans over and whispers in Finley's ear, "But I think I'll stick with princess. It seems to suit you better."

ABOUT THE AUTHOR

GEORGIA CATES

Georgia resides in rural Mississippi with her wonderful husband, Jeff, and their two beautiful daughters. She spent fourteen years as a labor and delivery nurse before she decided to pursue her dream of becoming an author and hasn't looked back yet.

Sign-up here to join the monthly newsletter for Georgia Cates. You will get the latest news, first-look teasers, and giveaways just for subscribers.

For the latest updates from Georgia Cates, stay connected with her at:

 @georgiacates

 georgia.cates.9

www.georgiacates.com

authorgeorgiacates@gmail.com

THE Beauty SERIES

THE SIN TRILOGY

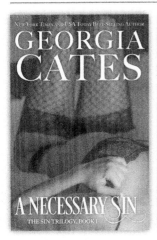

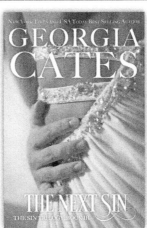

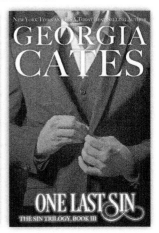

New York Times and USA Today Best-Selling Author
GEORGIA CATES

THE VAMPIRE AGÁPE SERIES